Escape to Other Earth

"Sis! SIS!"

No answer at all. No sound but the wind and the river and a night bird—maybe an owl—sleepily crying. It was as though my sister had disappeared from earth.

I was baffled. Verity wasn't in the water. I stared at the place where the stepping-stone was missing. At the reflection of the moon on the racing river, blazing, not being budged.

And then I knew. The reflection of the silver moon looked just like a moonlit stone coated with ice. With her dim eyesight, Verity had mistaken the moon on the water for a stepping-stone. Trustingly, she had set foot on the seventh stone—the moon—and now she was gone.

A furious snarling came from behind my back. Eager to get me, Rouser had tiptoed out as far as the second stone. Now he was crouching, a paw lifted, getting ready to spring toward me.

I had to decide. Fast. *Which would it be—the dog or the river?*

X. J. Kennedy THE OWLSTONE CROWN

Illustrated by Michele Chessare

BANTAM BOOKS
TORONTO · NEW YORK · LONDON · SYDNEY · AUCKLAND

RL 6, 008–013

THE OWLSTONE CROWN
A Bantam Book / published by arrangement with Atheneum Publishers, Inc.

PRINTING HISTORY
Atheneum edition published October 1983.
A Margaret K. McElderry book.

Bantam Skylark edition / October 1985

Skylark Books is a registered trademark
of Bantam Books, Inc. Registered in U.S.
Patent and Trademark Office and elsewhere.

All rights reserved.
Text copyright © 1983 by X. J. Kennedy.
Illustrations copyright © 1983 by Michele Chessare.
This book may not be reproduced in whole or in part, by
mimeograph or any other means, without permission.
For information address: Atheneum Publishers,
Div. of The Scribner Book Companies, 597 Fifth Avenue,
New York, N.Y. 10017.

ISBN 0-553-15349-8

Published simultaneously in the United States and Canada

Bantam Books are published by Bantam Books, Inc. Its trademark, consisting of the words "Bantam Books" and the por-
trayal of a rooster, is Registered in U.S. Patent and Trademark
Office and in other countries. Marca Registrada. Bantam
Books, Inc., 666 Fifth Avenue, New York, New York 10103.

For Kate, Dave, and Matt,
who kept asking,
"When are you going to write down
the story of the Moonflower?"
and for Dan and Josh as well

Contents

THE
OWLSTONE
CROWN

1. *A Detective Calls*

Ice. Ice everyplace. It made the branches of trees creak in the wind like hinges that hadn't been oiled. The snow wore a hard, bright crust. Every step you took mashed a spiderweb of cracks in it. That afternoon would have been great for skating, if we'd had skates, but instead we were out in the fields, my sister and I, trying to loosen some winter parsnips.

There was this one stubborn old vegetable. I dug around it, kicked it, but it wouldn't budge. I was jimmying my spade in under it, chipping at the frozen dirt, when—

TWAN-NN-NG-G-G!

A half-moon of iron snapped off and left me holding the handle of a spade that all of a sudden didn't have any point to it.

"Well, it isn't *your* fault, Timmy," said my sister.

"What do they expect? To make us dig parsnips in January!"

But I was scared to my bones. Paw Grimble was going to kill me for sure. A new spade would cost him seven dollars and ninety-eight cents. I knew it would, to the penny, because Paw was forever running on about the price of everything.

"Sis," I begged, "knock the dirt off those parsnips, will you? If we go home with an empty basket Paw will be TWICE as mad. And Maw won't give us any supper."

"Oh, who wants their old supper anyway? What do you bet it's parsnip stew again?"

Her forecast sounded likely. In the almost two hundred days we had been living with Maw and Paw Grimble—as they'd told us to call them—they must have fed us a hundred and fifty parsnip stews.

NOTE BY VERITY TIBB: *A hundred fifty-four. I kept count.*

You can see what a stickler for facts my sister is. All the while I'm telling this story, she'll probably keep putting in her fussy little two cents. Anyhow, the Grimbles weren't much on eating. Saving money was more in their line. They had fetched us out of the orphanage because they had needed two kids to work on their farm in Metal Horse, New Jersey, close to the Delaware Water Gap. They made medicine out of parsnips and sold it by mail. Maybe you've seen ads for it in

all the TV-star and soap-opera magazines—
GRIMBLE'S PARSNIP PUNCH FOR ABDOMINAL PRES-
SURE, THE SWEETHEART OF SEVENTY THOUSAND
SUFFERERS. Once I sneaked a gulp of the stuff.
Exploding dynamite would have tasted better.

NOTE BY VERITY TIBB: *Exaggerating. Always exaggerating. Making mountains out of mouseholes. That's
my brother, as usual. Watch out for him.*

Glumly, I picked up my shortened spade and
tried to loosen another parsnip. Verity, on her
hands and knees, felt around till she located the
last vegetable I had tossed her. She thumped it
on the frozen ground till its dirt fell off. That
was her part of the job. She couldn't see the parsnips well enough to dig them. All she could ever
see was the shapes of things.

We struggled on. All of a sudden a dirty parsnip whizzed past my left ear. Verity hadn't been
aiming for me, she was just letting go of her feel-
ings.

"YEE-EE-E-K-K!" she screamed, "I can't stand
any more of this!" And she plunked down onto
a snowbank.

With a sigh, I collapsed next to her. The wind
whistled between its teeth. A passing crow jeered
down at us.

Verity was tucking her long brown hair back
up under her knitted cap, and with her handkerchief, she was scrubbing frost from her thick,
glass-doorknob glasses. "Timmy," she said in her

best wheedling voice, "let's go play in the bear cave, why don't we?"

She'd been born twelve minutes ahead of me. That's why she was always trying to tell me what to do.

NOTE BY VERITY TIBB: *Well, back then, Timmy was such a cowardly sap. He never would have figured out what to do if somebody hadn't told him.*

For once I resisted. "Only a few more parsnips, Sis. Let's finish. It's getting dark."

"Timothy Tibb, I hate you! You're a boring drudge and I'm going to beat you up!"

And sweeping me off my feet with a cross-ankle pickup, she dropped me to my back and pinned me in a half-nelson. She was girls' wrestling champ of Walter B. Pitkin Junior High.

With kneeled-on chest, I lay helpless in the snow, staring at the white peak of Mount Peewee-hockey on the skyline. It looked like a head facing left, with a big bump for a nose.

"It's dull!—dull!—dull! around here," said Verity, kneeing me in the stomach with every *dull*. "I'm sick and tired of weeding parsnips"—knee-bump—"and pulling up parsnips"—knee-bump—"and shaking dirt off 'em!" She glowered down at me with magnified eyes.

"Ugh," I grunted, "do you—have to—murder me?"

"YES! I am The Strangler! I kill little boys! I'm

going to grind you up and feed you to the parsnips!"

"Look out, Sis, don't scratch your nose. You'll crush it."

"Crush what? My nose?"

"No. That ladybug."

"Liar!" Another knee landed in my stomach. "There aren't any ladybugs in January."

I managed to work a hand loose and bring it up to her nose. A spotted ladybug lifted the covers from its wings and flew down onto my outstretched finger.

"Now it's on me," I told her.

"Oh sure," my sister said. In a taunting voice she recited the old nursery rhyme:

Ladybug, ladybug, fly away home!
Your house is on fire and your children will burn!

Now comes the part of this story that sounds crazy. Even now, I can hardly believe it myself.

"Skip the wisecracks, angel," rasped a tiny voice. "I don't keep house and I don't have kids. If you must know, I'm a bachelor."

NOTE BY VERITY TIBB: *My brother can be an awful exaggerator, only this time he's right. That's exactly what the voice said. I remember, because I was so surprised I fell over backwards in the snow.*

Slowly and carefully I picked myself up, the ladybug still clinging to my finger. My hand in its glove was trembling so hard you'd think I was

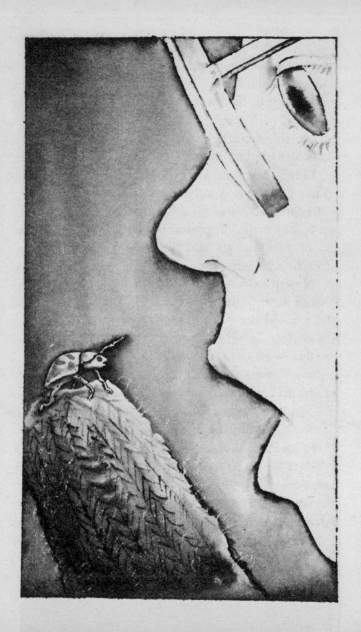

waving goodbye. The little beetle didn't look different from any other ladybug I'd known. Black and red, with seven spots. Now it was pacing around and around my finger, its head down, its rear end raised in the air.

"Did—did you say something?" I stammered.

"What's the matter?" came the same small voice with a buzz in it. "You have wax in your ears? Aren't you Timothy Tibb, age almost thirteen, and isn't this doll with the punk sense of humor your sister Verity?"

"How did you know our names?"

"Had 'em on file. You see, chum, I've been hired by your grandmother to check up on you."

"Don't joke," I pleaded. "Our grandmother is dead, and so is our grandfather. They drowned at sea off Cape May a year ago."

"No, they didn't," said the ladybug flatly. "They're alive and in pretty good shape for anybody locked in the slammer. I'm supposed to find you, see, and tell you so."

Gran and Gramp alive! How can I tell you what that news meant to us? We didn't have any mother or father, you understand. They had died when Verity and I were babies. I could barely remember my mother. A warm and fuzzy feeling when she had tucked a blanket around me on a cold night—that was all I had left of her. Anyhow, our grandparents were just the greatest people. Gramp built wonderful kites and hang-gliders, but mainly he was a philosopher. He'd written a book called *The Light to Live By* and he'd had it printed, but I don't believe anyone ever bought a copy. We would have gone hungry, I guess, if Gran hadn't taken to painting pictures and got good at it.

Gramp's last project had been a catamaran— a sailboat with two hulls joined side by side. When he had it all built, he had trucked it to the shore. I won't ever forget that day. The catamaran had lain along its pier, varnished and shining in the late afternoon sun. Gramp, wearing a captain's hat, had lifted a hand to Gran, and she, in a new sailor suit, had stepped into one swaying hull as proud as a queen. Then Gramp had hoisted the sails and the boat had skimmed out of the harbor and dwindled and dropped out of sight. Verity and I had stayed on the pier waiting for our promised ride while the sky had slowly reddened and grown dark and a full moon had risen. At last, after we told the police, a Coast Guard cutter with searchlights went looking for them. But they had just disappeared, as if they had dropped through a trapdoor, and the cutter hadn't found a trace of them.

"If," I said to the ladybug, "just IF our grandparents are still alive, where are they? What do you mean, they're in the slammer? Are they prisoners?"

"Rats!" said the ladybug harshly, "I can't stand here yapping. Us ladybugs can't stand cold climates. I've been on your freezing planet a long time—too long—checking every farm for miles around. OK, so I've found you. You've got your message. It's supposed to make you feel better and you're not to worry. Now so long—keep your noses clean!"

And he lifted his wing-cases to fly away.

"Hold on!" shrieked Verity at my elbow. "Who are you, anyway?"

"Ten above zero," groaned the bug, "and this doll has to have identification. OK, beautiful—look, here's my business card."

With a forefoot, he stuck out a white speck no bigger than a grain of sugar.

"I can't read it," said Verity.

"What's the matter?" snarled the bug. "Don't they teach you anything?" Then all of a sudden his voice softened. "Oh. Excuse me, kid. At first I didn't catch on to your eye problem. Maybe this palooka brother of yours will read the card for you."

"It's too little for me," I said.

Our visitor sounded annoyed. "Do I have to do everything for you? Lucky I come with a magnifying glass. Here, buster, take a squint through my left rear wingtip. Hurry up, this freezing cold makes me want to hibernate."

The wing was transparent, and as I stared through it, the white speck on my fingertip became a card with printed lettering. I read it aloud to Verity:

LEWIS O. LADYBUG

Private Investigator

Office: Moonflower (fourth blossom from the top)

Missing persons   Wandering child jobs

Low rates   Quick reports   Totally confidential

"Got me?" snapped the detective. "Now, boy, if you'll kindly move your ears out of the way, I'll be off. Hey! What are you doing? Let go of me!"

Lewis O. Ladybug was cornered. Just as he had begun to lift off from my little finger, I had lightly brought my thumb down on his back. I held him the way a jeweler studies a pearl.

"Maybe you had better go on talking," I told him, looking him straight in his compound eyes. "What's all this about our grandparents being prisoners?"

The little detective wriggled in my grip. "Buster," he snarled, "are you trying to get yourself a wooden overcoat?"

"Do you want a squeeze?" I bluffed.

"Go easy with that fat thumb of yours," he said threateningly. But reluctantly, he told us a little more. Our grandparents, catamaran and all, had dropped through a door into some other world. Now they were the prisoners of a dictator.

"Take us there," pleaded my sister, "so we can rescue them."

"Angel," said the bug with a sigh, "what chance would you kids have against a whole army of stone owls? Even if you *could* get to your grandfolks, you couldn't rescue them. Those owls are like rubber tires. They'd roll right over you."

"*We*'ll worry about that," I told him. "Either you help us find Gran and Gramp or I pinch you flat. Which?"

"Then I guess you pinch me, Fat Thumb. Your grandma gave me strict orders to keep you here on Earth and out of trouble. She's my client and I don't let a client down."

"Show us the door to this Other Earth," I said grimly.

"Nothing doing, buster. I'm not showing you any such door. Not today, not tomorrow, no time. Go ahead and pinch."

What a brave little guy! I really admired him. I lifted my thumb off his back and set him free.

"All right, Lewis O. Ladybug," I said. "Thanks for the message. You can go on back where you came from. And if you see our grandparents, please tell them—oh, I don't know. Tell them we miss them something fierce."

Still clinging to my fingertip, the bug fluttered

cramped wings. "OK. Only, come to think of it, I can't go back there yet. The nearest door won't open till the moon comes out. You kids wouldn't know where I could find me a couple of aphids, would you? Plant lice, you call 'em. That's my meat."

Verity wrinkled her brow. "Maybe you'd find some on Maw Grimble's cactus plant. Want to come inside with us and find out?"

The wind had sharpened its edge. The detective didn't need coaxing. Skimming along ahead of me, sometimes lighting on my coat-collar, he kept us company as we crunched across the snow back to the farmhouse, to the people I dreaded— me stumbling and bumping into trees because the light was dim, Verity sprinting and bounding because to her the darkness didn't much matter. I carried a new, wild hope and my broken spade and our half-empty parsnip basket.

2. *We Plot an Escape*

The farmhouse, like Maw and Paw Grimble themselves, looked worn-down and awful. Loose sideboards, their paint fallen away, stuck out all over it. That house always made me think of some bony old horse in need of combing.

I stood my pointless spade up against the cement block that served for a back doorstep. I wasn't about to mention my seven-dollar-and-ninety-eight-cent accident. All too soon, Maw or Paw would happen on the wreckage. Already I was twitching with cold dread.

NOTE BY VERITY: *See what I mean? About how my brother used to be a cowardly twerp?*

I'll admit it. Back in those days, I was scared of the Grimbles—and of everything else. I didn't climb trees for fear I would fall. To avoid meeting a strange dog I'd walk six blocks out of my way, and once, on hearing a bat twittering overhead,

I dived under a parked station wagon. I was a bundle of fears, all right. But I was working on them.

"Don't let the Grimbles see you, Lew," I whispered to the red dot on my coat collar.

"Right, kid—I'll lay low," came his rasp.

Nervously, I jiggled open the back door. Maw Grimble in her gray apron, her bent-wire masher in hand, was hunched over the stove, boiling something.

"What kept you two all this time?" she shrieked while Verity and I were stomping the snow off our boots and hooking up our coats and hats. She let out another, fiercer shriek when I set down our half-empty basket.

"Is that all the 'snips you got dug this afternoon? Didn't you finish them twelve rows like Paw told you to?"

"Finished all but eight, Maw," said my sister brightly.

"Daydreaming again!" Maw Grimble bellowed. Her bent-wire masher shot out and bopped Verity on one ear, then it shot out again and bopped me. "I declare," Maw went on, "you kids ain't worth the eats I keep wasting on you. Here I been standing on my sore feet fixing this nourishing parsnip stew, and poor Paw has been wearing his head to the bone figuring how to improve business. And all afternoon you kids have been having a fine time lallygagging around in the fresh air. Now you set down at that table and get them labels licked. Paw needs a load of bottles to take to the express office Monday morning."

Most of the kitchen table was taken up with bottles awaiting labels. Verity and I slumped into our chairs—mine had only three legs—while Maw hovered over us, fussing. I lifted a sheet of labels from a stack and ripped a label off and licked its back and stuck it on a bottle. Then I lowered the finished product into a pasteboard box.

Lew Ladybug took off from my collar and began touring the room. Verity and I kept working, not saying anything. My chair was trying to keel over onto its missing leg.

"Look out, boy!" Maw's masher pointed to the label I was sticking. "You've put a dirty fingerprint in the middle of it! Why didn't you wash your hands? Go do it. Then you clean off that label with the eraser."

As I was rinsing my hands in the kitchen sink, Lewis O. Ladybug sailed down, lit on a can of Ajax, and demanded, "What's the old turkey mad about?"

"Me," I muttered. "She always is."

"Talking behind my back, are you?" Maw thundered. A fresh blow of her masher clipped my ear—this time, my other one. That was the one nice thing about Maw. She always gave both ears equal time. The wind from her blow caught the ladybug by surprise. He went swirling into the air. After that, he cruised away and made himself scarce.

From her post at the gas stove, Maw kept jawing at us. Her tight gray hair bun wobbled as she punished the boiling parsnips with stabs of her masher. Despite the heat thrown by the stove, the kitchen was so cold you could see your breath. Once in a while the spiders, on their webs in the corners of the room, had to run around to keep from freezing solid.

On the wall I faced there was a battleship-gray cuckoo clock that said SOUVENIR OF OCEAN GROVE, N.J. Years ago the cuckoo had decided to give up and stay in hiding. Just over the clock, suspended by a tire-chain, was the potted cactus. I could see Lew crawling around on one of its dusty spikes, his red back the brightest thing in the household.

As we worked, Verity said in an undertone, "Timmy, are you thinking what I'm thinking?"

"How should I know?" I whispered. "Unless you're thinking we ought to trail the ladybug and find the door to this Other Earth. Are you thinking anything crazy like that?"

"You bet I am! The ladybug will stay here till the moon comes out. By that time, Maw and Paw will be sound asleep. We can escape! We can follow him!"

"But suppose we find that door? Wouldn't it be—uh—dangerous to go through it?"

"Timothy Tibb, if you aren't a chicken! Do you want to stay here with the Grimbles all your life? You want to come with me and rescue Gran and Gramp, don't you?"

An angry twittering on my shoulder made me jump.

"I heard you," rasped the detective. "Now get this straight. What's on the far side of that door is bad medicine. Worse than Parsnip Punch. You're staying right here. Oh, don't think for a minute that you guys can tail me. I'm an old pro at giving people the slip."

"Don't worry, Lew," I assured him. "*I* don't want to go to Other Earth. Honest, I don't."

But my voice had been louder than I had intended. Maw Grimble whirled around and raised her masher. I braced myself for a fresh bop on the ear, but she muttered something about me losing my mind, always talking to myself, and went back to beating up her parsnips. The ladybug flew back to his cactus.

Verity kicked me under the table and shot me a look that told me I was a caterpillar. She didn't care, it seemed—she still wanted to be a heroine.

"No more gabbing," Maw warned. "Keep lapping them labels while I take Rouser his supper."

Rouser was Paw Grimble's hunting dog—half hound, half timberwolf—and I lived in terror of him. His ribs stuck out, his back was covered with scabs. If you stepped up to his cage and tried to talk to him he'd snarl and bare his teeth and throw his body at you so hard he'd almost break the chicken wire of his cage. Maw was holding a dish of beef bones, cooked, with plenty of juicy meat on them. It looked so much better than the parsnip stew we were in for that I felt like racing the dog for it. Maw flung a scarf around her neck and barged outside. Now she would see the broken spade. I was a goner!

Sure enough. The second she returned from the dog's cage, she let out her best shriek ever. The back door bashed open again and in she

strode, holding the rusty spade like a terrier shaking a rat.

At the sight of her blazing eyes, I completely panicked. I lost my grip on the three-legged chair. The thing pitched over sideways, dumping me off, and I slid in under the kitchen table. There I lay, flat on my back, while loose labels snowed all around me. PARSNIP PUNCH, said the flakes. THE SWEETHEART OF 70,000 SUFFERERS.

"Paw! You, Paw!" Maw Grimble screamed. "You come in here this minute and see what this fool boy has done to your brand new spade!"

All afternoon while we had been working in the fields, Paw Grimble had been dozing in his rocking chair in the parlor. Maw's screams had wakened him, and soon his checkered slippers appeared out beyond the hanging edge of the plastic tablecloth. He stooped down and peered in on me. His bald skull was as gray as a burned-out light bulb.

He studied me from in back of his steel-rimmed glasses. "Boy, what are you doing in under there?"

"Just thinking how to improve business, Paw," I quavered.

One of his bony fists gathered my shirtfront into a knot and hauled me out and stood me on my feet.

"Now what's this about a spade?" he wanted to know.

"He broke it," Maw said, sniveling, shaking the pointless spade under Paw's nose.

"*WHAT?*" Paw's glasses sparkled angrily. "SEVEN DOLLARS AND NINETY-EIGHT CENTS PLUS TAX. Boy, can you understand how much MONEY that is?"

I just shook in my shoes.

"ANSWER ME!"

"Well," I said lamely, "it's two cents short of eight dollars."

My answer turned him purple in the face. "I could thrash you, boy. Thrash you within an inch of your life."

I didn't expect he would beat me. That would have meant work for him.

"You're going to pay," he bleated. "You're going to stick extra labels. Every ten extra labels you stick, you'll make a cent. That's seven thousand nine hundred and eighty labels you can stick, not counting the ones you have to stick anyway. You can get up every morning at three o'clock till you get 'em all stuck. And from now on you can go without breakfast."

Verity's wild plan to run away to Other Earth was looking better and better to me.

Supper, as you might expect, was pretty miserable. I managed to force down two or three bites of stew, all the time wishing I was a ladybug and could eat aphids. Verity sat at the table winding parsnip strings around her fork, which had lost all but two of its tines, and looking sick to her stomach. Paw, he kind of inhaled his stew the way a vacuum cleaner will suck up anything. Nobody talked except Maw. Between jawfuls of stew, she kept up a running complaint about me and that spade. You'd have thought I had murdered her cousin.

"Now, after supper," she went on, "you kids clean your shoes. Use your toothbrushes, only wash 'em out real good afterwards. Always walk with your feet flat on the ground so your shoes will wear out even. Verity, have you been saving them little gummed paper strips off of the postage stamps? Never can tell when they might come in handy. Timothy, pinch your nose so you don't sneeze. Sneezing wears out handkerchiefs. Verity, why ain't you eating your good supper?"

"Aw, Maw, I can't get it down tonight. I'm afraid I'll choke on it."

"Uppitty girl," Maw said with a sniff. "Never do appreciate anything. I suppose you wish you was back with your old grandfolks again, eating chicken and ice cream and rich junk like that. But your grandfolks is dead, child, deader than doornails. Why, you'd still be in the orphan house if Paw and me hadn't had the kindness to take you in. Ain't you grateful, girl, for the loving care and nourishing food and nice clothes we been giving you?"

"Well, no, Maw, now that you ask, I can't say

I'm grateful a bit. This parsnip pulp isn't worth eating. Couldn't you give us a carrot once in a while? And our clothes aren't nice. They're old holey hand-me-downs you fish out of other people's garbage."

You can imagine how *that* speech landed. Maw's jaw dropped. Her eyeballs bulged like a couple of soft-boiled eggs.

To my despair, Verity kept on talking. "Sure you feed us—sort of—and the State of New Jersey sends you a check for doing it. We don't get much to eat, so you must have a lot of money left over."

Whack!

Maw placed a slap across my sister's mouth that knocked her thick glasses flying.

"Don't you dare say that," Maw warned in a low, quivering voice. "Don't you ever say that when the lady from the State comes snooping around checking up on us, you hear?"

Verity looked determined not to cry. I retrieved her glasses for her. Maw carried on and on about why didn't the State send them some hard-working kids for a change instead of a blinky with too much mouth and a boy that couldn't dig parsnips without destroying property. I was growing so mad I was almost forgetting to be scared of her. And all this time Paw Grimble kept his steely eyes drilling at the ceiling, a mean smile tugging his lip corners.

We didn't get a minute's peace till the dishes had been put away and Verity and I were back to sticking labels. I nudged my sister under the table to let her know that now I was on her side. I'd run away with her. But every once in a while my common sense would return, and I'd start shuddering. Did our scheme really have any chance? The ladybug suspected us. How could we hope to follow him?

From their parlor the Grimbles could see out into the kitchen and could police us while we worked. In a stiff-backed chair, Maw was soaking her feet in a bucket of water and baking soda. Paw, in his creaky rocker, twisted the old black-and-white TV to his favorite program. It was a game show played in a supermarket. The idea of it was to heap a shopping cart with as many groceries as you could grab in so many minutes. The program repeated itself a lot, and Paw knew every show by heart. "Look, Maw," he cackled, "here's the one where the lady from Pasadena don't take nothing but them nine-dollar canned hams."

Verity, trying to cheer herself, was humming. "Stop that!" Maw called.

His TV show over, Paw snapped off the set and declared that tonight he felt considerable pressure on his abdomen. He came out into the kitchen and grabbed six bottles of punch that we hadn't labeled yet. Then he shuffled back into the parlor and just sipped and rocked, rocked and sipped. Now and again he'd burp.

Lewis O. Ladybug, looking rounder and heavier, skimmed down to the top of a bottle I was identifying. "Rubberiest old aphids I ever ate," he said wolfishly.

"Listen, Lew," I pleaded, "you've got to take us with you to Other Earth. You can't leave us here! Don't you see what the Grimbles are like?"

"They're a bum scene," admitted the detective. "But at least, living with them, you'll stay alive."

A skinny shadow fell across our table. I glanced up to see Paw, a bottle of punch in his hand, standing over us, swaying.

"Who are you kids talking to?" he wanted to know.

"This ladybug," said Verity matter-of-factly.

My heart just about froze. If only my sister could tell a little white lie once in a while! I don't know why she couldn't. She just hated to. And we were always getting into trouble as a result.

Paw lowered his nose to the bottlecap Lew was sitting on. "Ladybugs don't talk," he said thickly.

"Oh, don't they?" said the detective evenly. "I know your type, Grimble. All you are is a cheap two-bit slave-driver. I ought to replace your teeth, but I never pick on a drunk. Now get back to your rocking chair and suck your homemade poison before I twist that ugly beak of yours into a knot."

With a gasp, Paw drew back his nose. For a

moment I thought he was going to crush his hand down on the little detective. He looked as pale as if a vampire had just guzzled him.

Then, to my relief, he straightened up, staggered to the sink, and poured in what was left of his bottleful.

"Maw," he said in a hollow voice, "I believe I'll need to correct the strength of what's down cellar in the vat. This new batch is a mite too powerful."

If Verity and I could have laughed, we'd have had hysterics. We had to cram our knuckles into our mouths, and for a long time we didn't dare look at each other.

By and by, when I could risk a glance into the parlor, both Paw and Maw had their heads down on their chests and were breathing like a couple of leaky accordions.

Through the window over the sink, the moon was blazing, yellow and round as the center of a giant daisy.

"Time to take off, chums," said Lew Ladybug. "So long. Keep your chins in the air. Don't take any wooden nickels."

And he darted off through a crack under the back door.

"Quick, grab your coat!" I whispered to Verity.

But I must have whispered too loud. Maw Grimble woke up with a snort.

"You ain't going no place," she said.

3. *The Seventh Step*

Maw Grimble's words landed on my ears like blows from her terrible masher. Verity and I fell to labeling bottles again, like a couple of good robots, but on the inside, I was boiling with frenzy. Now the ladybug was gone. Flying away. Soon he'd be forever lost to us.

"See you don't use too much spit on them labels," Maw advised. "Your tongues will go dry and you'll want a drink, and water costs good money..."

Her voice mumbled away. And then—great snakes and little green hoptoads, didn't our luck improve, because the next sound out of her was a beautiful big fat snore.

We didn't waste any more time. We jumped from our chairs, flung on our coats and hats, and not bothering with overshoes, inched toward the back door. My heart was slamming my ribs. As we eased past the stove, moving slowly and carefully so the floorboards wouldn't creak, Maw gave a new snort. For an instant we stood there petrified, me with one foot in the air, but soon Maw fell back to the land of dreams, so I lowered my foot and worked open the door and held it wide for Verity. Without a sound, we stepped out into the January night.

Verity let out her breath. "All right, Eagle-eyes, where's the ladybug?"

The moon on the ice-covered snow made the back yard blaze. On the leafless trees, every twig stood out. But I couldn't see the detective. He was too small. Or had he—after our delay—already taken off for Other Earth?

And then, hardly a stone's toss from us, a bat dived for something in the air.

"Beat it," a voice rasped, "before I poke you one."

The bat gave a twitter and flew away, no doubt surprised at having a bite of food talk back to it.

"There he is!" I cried—too loudly. Rouser must have pricked up his ears. From his cage by the side of the barn, he gave a piercing whine.

Verity's green eyes, looking huge behind glass, threw me a hopeless stare. "That dog will wake Maw and Paw!"

A slam. A groan of boards. The mean mutt

had bombed himself against his chicken wire. A thud. He had dropped back to make a second charge.

From inside the house, Paw Grimble's voice rang out. "Whatsa matter, Rouser? Somebody out there, boy?"

I was desperately keeping my eyes fixed on the ladybug. He was flying along the path, with the moonlight glinting on his wings.

"He's heading for the woods!" I cried.

Verity and I broke into a run. She could run faster than I could, any day. She knew every tree and pebble on that farm. Skidding and sliding on the glass-topped snow, we charged down the path and rounded the barn, following the ladybug, while the wolf-dog bounded and howled.

But the detective could fly faster than we could run, and by the time we got to the edge of the woods, we had lost him in among the trees.

From the farmhouse came the noise of Paw stumbling around, cussing and bumping into things. No doubt looking for his shotgun. By this time, Rouser was howling like a stuck steam whistle.

"Into the woods!" I cried. "Come on, Sis, let's do the coat-tail!"

NOTE BY VERITY: *The coat-tail was our method of steering me whenever we had to travel fast through woods or through someplace I wasn't familiar with. I'd grab the back of Timmy's coat and we'd run. That's how we traveled together.*

We barged into a thicket. The ladybug, I figured, would keep to the main path, the shortest way through the woods. We'd avoid the path, so he wouldn't see us. The woods closed in around us. Behind our backs, the Grimble farm dropped away like a bad dream.

But soon, from the rim of the woods, came a dog's baying, followed by the steady *crunch, crunch, crunch* of bootsteps in the snow.

"After 'em, boy!" Paw Grimble was bawling. "Don't let 'em get away!"

I tugged Verity down behind a thorn bush. The baying and the crunching drew near. Now we could hear the click of Rouser's toenails on the crusty snow and Paw's mutter, "When I catch them kids, they'll skip a month of suppers, they will..." Butterflies were beating around in my stomach. No, they were pterodactyls.

Luckily, the wind was aiming straight for us, so that Rouser, running the other way, didn't pick up our scent. We stayed down till Paw and the dog had passed, then we got up and moved on through the underbrush as quietly as possible. Still, the creaking of snow under my feet sounded louder to me than fire sirens.

For a long time we went around in circles, getting scratched by brambles and twigs. At last I stopped, and Verity, clinging to my coat-tail, slammed into me.

"What's the matter? Why are we stopping?" she demanded.

"I don't see the ladybug," I admitted. "I don't know which way to go."

"Dumbhead! Bubble-brain!" she exploded, while I dodged her attempts to strangle me. "You've let the ladybug get away? What have we been running around in these scratchy bushes for, the last half-hour?"

"Sorry, Sis. Finding a ladybug in the woods at night isn't the easiest thing in the world, you know."

"So *you* say. Oooh, if only *I* could see better!"

Then, from out of the thicket near us, came the crashing and bashing of the dog. The wind had shifted. Rouser had picked up our trail!

"For heaven's sake, Timmy! Let's not stand here! Aren't we close to the river? I can hear it gurgling. Come on! If we cross to the other side, we'll lose that dog!"

The river *was* nearby. It was a deep stream that came racing down out of the hills fast enough to keep flowing and not freezing even in January. Stepping-stones led across it in a chain maybe twenty feet long.

"Come on!" my sister urged me, when we'd got to the river's shore. Hoisting her pants legs to keep them dry, she fastened a sneakered foot down on the first stepping-stone.

"Those stones are covered with ice. Won't we slip?"

She gave me a sniff of contempt. Sure-footed as a mountain goat, she was hopping from stone to stone across the rushing water.

"ARRR-OO-OO-OOO!"

That howl made me whirl. From the bushes along shore came a furious crackling and smashing, then Rouser's lowered head and bony forelegs broke through. He looked at me. He froze. The moonlight made his teeth and eyeballs glow. I felt like a cornered rabbit.

Maybe I'd follow Verity. I stepped down onto the first round stone—the second stone—the third. By the light of the moon, the ice on the stones looked silver. Once, I slipped and got a wet foot, but I kept going. When I came to stone number six, I met a gap in the chain where I'd have to jump—oh, for maybe a yard. Where the seventh stone ought to have been, the reflection of the full moon blazed on the speeding water.

But where was Verity? Had she already crossed? In the moonlight, everything looked sharp and exact, as if somebody had traced all around it with a pencil. I scanned the opposite shore, but I couldn't see a sign of Verity.

"Sis?" I called.

No answer.

"Sis! SIS!"

No answer at all. No sound but the wind and the river and a night bird—maybe an owl—sleepily crying.

It was as though my sister had disappeared from earth.

I was baffled. Verity wasn't in the water. I stared at the place where a stepping-stone was missing. At the reflection of the moon on the racing river, blazing, not being budged.

And then I knew. The reflection of the silver moon looked just like a moonlit stone coated with ice. With her dim eyesight, Verity had mistaken the moon on the water for a stepping-stone. She'd been charging along, not counting. Trustingly, she had set foot on the seventh stone—the moon—and now she was gone.

A furious snarling came from behind my back. Eager to get me, Rouser had tiptoed out as far as the second stone. Now he was crouching, a paw lifted, getting ready to spring on to stone number three.

I had to decide. Fast. Which would it be—the dog or the river?

To tell you the truth, I didn't much care for either. And yet I lifted my right foot and just as Verity had done, stepped down on the seventh stone. On the moon in that hurrying stream.

The water blurred. The reflected moon swayed under me. It loomed bigger than any moon I'd seen before.

I was falling. Falling into the moon.

The wolf-dog gave a disappointed howl.

4. *Our First Stone Owl*

I splashed down into deep water. I plunged in over my head, touched bottom, came up again. Warm water dwindled away from me as though a swimming pool I swam in was being drained. When my eyes opened, the river had shallowed down again. I was standing in water up over my ankles. Flowing water. The wet familiar stepping-stones gleamed under the moon.

I was on Other Earth, I knew suddenly, and yet nothing looked different. *Nothing?* I took a closer look. No ice on the river's stepping-stones, no snow along its shores. The air was as warm as an electric blanket. Overhead, a weak and hazy moon was fighting through a traffic-jam of clouds. It didn't seem right—the night sky in New Jersey had been *clear*.

Verity was sitting on the far bank of the river, hatless, coatless, her long hair stringing her face.

"Sis!" I cried, grateful to see her.

"Slowpoke. You took your time getting over here!"

"Well, at first I couldn't figure out where you'd gone."

"What do you mean? I didn't go anyplace. Except over the stepping-stones."

"Then how come you're all wet?"

"I slipped and fell in. What's happened to Rouser? Did he get lost?"

She didn't know where she was! Her weak eyes couldn't see that anything had changed. She hadn't yet registered the change in temperature. Setting foot on the last stone in the chain, I finally landed on the shore I had set out for in another world. My soaked coat weighted a ton, so I wiggled out of it. I slumped down next to Verity on the riverbank.

"Sis, don't you understand? We've done it. We've come through the door."

"Quit kidding, Timmy. For Pete's sake, I want to find the ladybug and go through the door just as much as you do. But it's nothing to kid me about."

On a nearby milkweed, a red-and-black speck had settled. It was shaking a drop of water from its wings.

"Think you're smart, do you?" the ladybug accused. "Well, you kids are in trouble. So am I,

when your grandmother finds out you've followed me."

Verity looked as if a lightning bolt had fallen
in her lap. "Lew, is that you? Then you mean we
really DID—?"

"Why don't you kids go back where you came
from?" the detective growled. "Hurry up, step
back through that moon on the river before the
door shuts. Before our moon and your moon
slide out of line. I'm telling you—this will be your
last chance for a month. Go on! That door will
stay open for a few minutes more."

"We're never going back," Verity said firmly.

"If we did," I put in, "Rouser would mangle
us."

"Lew, we're staying with you," said Verity as if
that was *that*.

The detective groaned. "Just my luck. A couple
of kids to look after. That's all I need."

A strange fact hit me. The ladybug was sitting
on a milkweed. Since when did milkweeds grow
in January? Only it wasn't January. There wasn't
any snow. All around us, crickets and tree toads
were making music. A warm, sweet-smelling wind
rustled leaves and scurried through the knee-deep
grass.

"Sis," I said in wonder, "do you know what?
It's summer!"

"Of course it is. Don't you think I can hear

crickets? But now I can hardly see *anything*."

I looked her in the face. Something was missing. "Sis, where are your glasses?"

"I don't know. They must have dropped off between Earth and Other Earth."

I turned to the milkweed. "Lew, is there any place around here that makes new glasses?"

"Naw," said the bug. "The kid needs glasses? Then why don't you both just walk out on those stepping-stones again and go back to that nice safe parsnip farm?"

"Glasses or no glasses, we're staying," Verity said. "Timmy can help me find my way around. We came here to rescue Gran and Gramp, you understand, so please take us to them."

"Hello, Lew, how's tricks?"

This greeting came from a ghostlike thing that had suddenly drifted toward us. It was a sort of moth the size of a kite. Two long feathery antennas wobbled on its brow, and as it flew, a pair of rainbow-colored wings revolved at its sides like a couple of paddlewheels. Lew greeted it in return—Dutch, he called it—and the beautiful moth flew on past us.

"That was a windmill moth," said the detective, starting to thaw a little. "Nice-looking, aren't they? There used to be millions of the things, but there aren't many any more. Not since that bum who calls himself Raoul Owlstone threw the dome over the Moonflower. Keeps the moths from drinking its juice. *Oh oh.* Here's trouble. DUTCH, LOOK OUT—!"

From out of the sky a batlike shape descended. It dived straight for the windmill moth and caught it in midair. The moth disappeared with a crunch like a bitten potato chip. Dark wings flapped as the hunter flew away with a terrible shriek that sounded like *"Meat! Eat meat!"*

Silence. A lonesome bird called sadly in the night.

"That was a muckhawk," Lew said at last. "One of Raoul's pets."

"Let's not meet any more of them," I said.

Suddenly the ladybug was staring through me, goggling his compound eyes. "Don't look now, kid," he said tonelessly, "but something a lot worse than a muckhawk is standing in back of you."

I turned around. I looked up and gasped.

The stone owl peered down at me with electric cells for eyes. They glowered, but didn't cast light. The owl looked like a statue made out of dark gray stone with a pattern like feathers all over it. It loomed above me, taller than a skyscraper.

NOTE BY VERITY: *Yeah—I'll bet!*

Stickler! That was how tall the owl looked to me at the moment, I mean. All right, it was about six feet six inches tall. It stood bolt upright on a ball of the same kind of gray, feathered stone. The ball was maybe fourteen inches across. The

owl traveled along on top of that rolling globe, just standing there while only the globe moved. Now it was flapping the lower half of its beak, and a flat machine-made voice came grating out—"State your names."

My mouth was dry. I couldn't say a word.

"Go on, answer it," the ladybug urged from my right shoulder.

"I—I'm Timothy Tibb," I stammered, "and this is my sister Verity. We're with Lewis O. Ladybug, Private Investigator."

"Reply unsatisfactory," droned the robot voice. "Ladybug is not a person. Delete."

"Delete who?" the detective snarled. "Where do you get that stuff? I'm a lot more of a person, buster, than you'll ever be. Why don't you go choke on an owlstone mouse?"

SNAP! The owl's beak made a swoop at my shoulder, but the detective had leaped to safety in the air.

"Names, Timothy Tibb and Verity Tibb," the owl went on. "State your places of residence."

"Oh, we don't live in this world," said Verity, "we live in Metal Horse."

"Residence, Metal Horse World. State your business."

"Please," I quavered, "we've come here to talk with Raoul Owlstone. He's keeping our grandmother and grandfather in jail, and we're going to ask him to let them go."

The owl's eye-cells glared. "Reply unsatisfactory. Our master does not speak to children. Our master never releases prisoners. You are unsatisfactory. You are under arrest. Stand where you are."

The ladybug, from my collar, let out a whistle. "I don't like this."

The owl lowered its head, which appeared to work on a hinge, and rummaged around under one stone wing. When its head snapped back up again it wore a thing shaped like a cone that fitted like a muzzle over its beak.

"Wouldn't you know," said Lew glumly, "it's calling headquarters. Looks like you're bound for the cooler, kids."

"V Q Twenty-Nine reporting," the owl droned. "Send stone egg at once to sector Thirty-One W. Two unsatisfactory persons without business." We were going to jail! For keeps! Never to find Gran and Gramp! Something inside me went wild. If I'd had time to think what I was doing, I wouldn't have done it, of course. The owl stood facing me, its back to the river. With all my might, I bombed myself into its chest. Its body felt cold, like a shark's. I'd caught the owl just right. It flipped over backwards with its big ball-bearing up in the air and lay on its spine, teetering, balanced on the closest stepping-stone. I couldn't stop now. Wading up to the owl, I cupped my hands under its stone tail and jerked up hard. The owl, like a log going down a chute in a lumbermill, slid neatly into the reflected moon on the water just off shore. Slid into the moon and was gone. The river sloshed and tilted in its bed.

From my shoulder, Lew gave a gasp. "Kid, that was beautiful! Sweet! You're a chip off your grandfather's block!" Then he recovered himself and growled, "Only you've made things worse. Just wait till the other owls find out."

The splash of the owl in the river hadn't been lost on Verity. Now she gave me a squeeze and said, "Timmy, I'm proud of you. But Lew, what will happen to that owl?"

"It'll take a trip. It'll shoot through to *your* earth like a cannonball."

"Then Timmy has turned a monster loose on Northern New Jersey?"

"Naw. Not for long, anyway. That owl's batteries ought to run down in a day or two. But when it first hits Earth, I wouldn't want to be the first one it meets."

"That will be Paw Grimble," I said. Somehow the notion of Paw meeting the stone owl in the woods cheered me greatly. Verity and I started to laugh and laugh.

"Stick around, you kids," the detective snarled, "and you'll be laughing out of the other sides of your mouths. Don't you understand? That owl put a call straight to headquarters, and there's a stone egg coming. In fact, it should be here right now."

A fit of the galloping shakes came over me. "Lew! You're our friend! Tell us—what'll we do?"

"Hide," said the detective.

"But where? We don't know this country."

"Sure you do, kid, you know this neighborhood better than anybody. Where would you hide if this was your old Earth?"

I thought fast. "Ummm. There's a little cave we used to play in. You mean—there's a cave just like it on *this* earth?"

"Right," said the detective, "haven't you noticed? Other Earth is shaped exactly the same as yours. Same rivers, mountains, everything. I know the cave you mean. It's the only cave for fifty miles around. Can you get to it?"

I nodded. In the distance I could see a familiar landmark. Mount Peeweehockey, with its big bump for a nose.

"Then MOVE, why don't you?" Lew urged. "Duck into that cave and lay low till the heat dies down. So long—I've got to report to your grandmother. Wish me luck. I'd rather face a couple of stone owls. In the morning I'll come meet you at the cave."

He spiraled away from my shoulder and was gone.

"Hee-hee-hee!" came a tittering laugh from the

nearby darkness. "I heard you! I saw everything!"

Startled, I jumped. The voice was a mean little peeping one. I looked around to see where it was coming from. Under the dim moon I could barely make out a little grayish-green blob on the trunk of the nearest pine. It was a tree toad about two inches long, the color of pine tree bark.

The toad threw me a wink. "I saw you push that owl into the river. Oh, don't worry, I won't tell. Not if you'll make your payments regularly."

"What do you want?" I asked.

"For a start, you could round me up, say, two hundred June bugs. That will be plenty for tonight. Then you can bring me two hundred every day for the next six weeks."

"Whoever you are, get lost!" shrilled Verity. "We came here to rescue Gran and Gramp, not to go bug-collecting."

"Hee-hee-hee! I know where you'll be hiding. In the cave on the side of the hill!"

"No, no," I denied, "we're not going there."

"What are you talking about, Timmy?" countered my sister. "Of course we are!"

I grabbed for the toad, but he was too quick for me. He skittered around to the far side of his tree trunk and flung back, "You'll be sorry!"

"Sis, you goof," I groaned, "why did you have to admit we're going to the cave? That toad will tell the owls on us for certain. Now we have to find a better place to hide."

"Know any?"

She had me. The cave was the only hiding place I knew. Unless we went there, how could Lew find us again? I thought I heard a roar from overhead.

We didn't wait around for the stone egg to come down and grab us—whatever a stone egg was. In a hurry, we struck out through the woods, following a path that seemed new to me. Still, I didn't have any trouble keeping my bearings, because the mountain on the skyline stayed in front of us.

As we ran, doing the shirt-tail through the underbrush, we passed a horrible sight. There was this house in a field, a house with cheerful red shutters, painted lately. Only it had been crushed. Smack in the middle of its roof sat a ball of mud as big as an elephant. Loose shingles strewed the yard. Next to a gate swinging idly in the wind, a mailbox stood, its flag lifted, lettered with the people's name, WEEDBLOSSOM. I guessed they didn't live there anymore.

The sight picked me up and made me run on faster. At last we came to the bear cave—that was our made-up name for it. It was a slot big enough for six or eight kids to fit into, in the side of a knobby hill. We scrambled inside and threw ourselves down on its hard, cool floor and let our breaths catch up with us.

Verity wrinkled her nose. "Phew-w-w-w," she

said, "it certainly smells worse than our cave in Metal Horse."

We sprawled on our backs and talked, and I tried to cheer us up. But Verity, with her usual bluntness, said, "Timmy, let's face it, we don't have much reason to be glad. Here we are—alone in some screwy world. Our clothes are wetter than dishrags and I've lost my glasses and now all I can see is a little bit of light. You'll have to look out for us both, and as you know, you're kind of incompetent. An army of owls is looking for us, and that tree toad is going to tell them where we are."

It was a pretty convincing list.

"We'll be all right," I said, but my words, hitting the ceiling of the cave, boomed hollowly.

In my shirt pocket I had a chocolate bar I'd been saving. Now I divided half of it with Verity and returned the other half to my pocket for another day. We munched, and my sister wondered about the doorway we had fallen through. I had it all figured out. The full moon had shone on our river in New Jersey, and on Other Earth, in a river just like ours, a door had opened. Gran and Gramp, I reasoned, must have dropped through a different door, one out in the Atlantic. Both earths must be sprinkled with such watery doors that needed a full moon to open them.

I rattled on and on, warming to my theories.

"Sis?" I said.

No answer. She was snoring. I lay there on the cave floor, my mind going around. Now that my sister had lost her glasses I would have to lead her around and find my own way besides. In the past she had always told me what to do. Now, I would have to think for myself. And that house crushed by the mudball—that bothered me. I thought of Gran and Gramp. It wasn't going to be easy to rescue them. Oh, why did I have to be such a coward? I was worried and scared, but I was also tired, tired to the bone, and soon a breaker of sleep washed over me.

I had a beautiful dream. Rouser, whining in terror, was clinging to a tree for dear life. A seven-foot-tall stone owl, clicking its beak, was chasing Maw and Paw Grimble around and around the frozen parsnip patch.

5. Cornered in a Cave

When you wake up to find a huge shaggy head bending over you, snuffling loudly, and you feel a cold nose exploring your shirtfront and bristly hairs rubbing your chin—oh, you think you're having a loser of a dream.

But I was awake. I wanted to yell and didn't dare to. I shut my eyes again and kept lying on my back, playing dead. The cold nose prowled my chest till it came to the pocket with the chocolate bar. Teeth tugged out the candy, and I could hear its wrapper being swatted off, then the sound of slow, heavy chomping.

I opened my eyelids a slit. By the weak light of dawn I could see the bear, a thick brown giant of a guy, easily nine feet tall. Done with his snack, he licked his claws thoughtfully with a long violet-colored tongue. Then he returned to me and sniffed my pants pockets, looking for a second helping. At last, to my relief, he gave up the search and lay down on his side, looking annoyed. I studied him. He had deep-set eyes, a sloping brow, small, rounded ears, and a short stiff beard under his chin. He was so big he practically blocked the mouth of the cave.

Verity was still sleeping. I'd have to face this shaggy monster on my own. Of course, I was scared silly. Desperate for some weapon, I glanced about. On the cave floor inches from my right hand lay a piece of tree branch about a foot long. My hand stole to it and closed around it.

I'd take him by surprise! Whipping the hunk of wood out in front of me, I jumped to my feet— bonking my head, because the cave wasn't as tall as I was—and I shook my weapon under the brown bear's nose.

"All right, you big crook," I glowered, keeping my voice as steady as I could, "get out of here! Beat it! Scat!"

NOTE BY VERITY: *Wasn't Timmy brave? Already, Other Earth was starting to improve him. Of course, he was dumb to take on a strange bear like that. Really stupid, you might say.*

The bear just looked at me as though I was a bothersome flea. Then, with insulting laziness, one shaggy paw came out and removed the stick from my hand, the way you'd take a toy away from a two-year-old, and dashed it to the floor.

His deep voice found words slowly. "This is *my* cave. Sit down. Don't be afraid."

I sat. There was something gentle about this bear. His soft voice took the fear out of me.

The wood hitting the floor had roused Verity. Now she was rubbing her eyes, squinting at the bear's dark, shaggy form.

"It's a bear, Sis," I explained.

"A BEAR?"

The owner of the cave looked at her. "You scared of me?"

"YES!" she shrieked.

"How come?"

"Because you have teeth and claws. Because you're going to bite my head off."

The bear seemed to quake all over, silently. "Your head wouldn't taste good," he boomed at last. "You kids hungry?"

"Starving," I admitted.

"Then have a fish."

A string of wet brook trout glittered on the cave's floor. Next to it stood a pail overflowing with blackberries and a honeycomb, thick and white. The bear had been out all night collecting grub.

"Uh—about the fish, no thanks," I faltered. "But we could use some berries and honey."

"Picky eaters, huh?" muttered the bear, with a help-yourself wave of a paw. Ripping a trout from the string, he stuffed it between his jaws. Another trout followed, and then another. As he polished off each fish, he would toss its head onto a pile of garbage at the back of the cave.

The blackberries were cold, as if their pail had been sitting in an icy spring. The honey, gritty as salt, filled your mouth with flowers. Verity and I hadn't had a meal that good in almost two hundred days. After breakfast, the three of us propped our backs against a cave wall and felt comfortable. The brown bear was licking off his nails, one at a time. Yellowish-white and curved they were, like shelled Brazil nuts.

He sighed. "Honey gets harder to find every day. The bees had to stop drinking from the Moonflower."

"Does everything in this country talk?" Verity wanted to know. "All the animals and bugs, I mean?"

"Not all of them," said the brown bear after some thought. "I knew an earthworm once who was kind of a blob. You could hardly get two words out of him. Who are you kids anyway?"

Briefly, I told him our story. Just for fun, I introduced Verity by her school nickname, which she hates.

"Hello, Terrible Verity," said the bear, while my sister took her revenge by yanking hairs out of my scalp. "They call me Fardels. That's what I'm always carrying—burdens—bundles of wood—and that's what Fardels means. I'm in the business, see?"

I hadn't noticed till now, but most of the cave's

walls were piled high with split logs and bundles of sticks. On the floor lay an ax in a heap of wood chips. At the entrance to the cave hung a small hand-lettered sign, which, in our haste to get into the cave the night before, had passed me completely by:

FARDELS BEAR
Firewood

Don't chop. Buy yours here.
Why grunt and sweat?

"Mustard Weedblossom made me that sign," the bear said proudly. "He's the kid who used to live in that busted farmhouse. I've been swapping wood with people for something to eat. Now that there isn't a zoo to feed me any more."

"Ouch!" I cried, as Verity uprooted a whole clump of my hair. "You're a zoo bear?"

"Used to be. I'm a Kodiak brown."

"*Yow!* Do you miss the zoo?"

"Sometimes. Mine was the biggest cage. Had my own swimming pool. Always had plenty of fish. Didn't have a thing to do except make people laugh. But that was before Raoul Owlstone!"

As he said the name of the Dictator, Fardels Bear gave a terrible growl and flashed his teeth. For a minute I thought he was going to tear the world apart. Just then came a tiny commotion in the air, and a familiar voice rasped, "Aw, can it, bear, all this yap about the good old days. On your feet, you kids! You need to blow this dump! Fast!"

"Lew!" cried my sister joyfully. "You've come back to us! Did you see Gran?"

"No time to shoot the breeze, baby," barked the detective from his perch on the bear's nose. "You've got to get out of here. Now!"

"What's the rush, Lew?" the bear wanted to know.

"Stone owls. A flock of 'em. They're searching for these kids and they're heading straight this way. Will you *move*, Tim and Verity?"

The ladybug's warning hadn't come too soon. From outside the cave, high in the air, came a grating mechanical voice over a loudspeaker. Its echoes scampered up and down the hillside:

BEAR!	BEAR!	BEAR!
WHERE	WHERE	WHERE
ARE BOY	BOY	BOY
AND GIRL	GIRL	GIRL?

"This is Peepy Treetoad's work," said Lew bitterly. "He ratted on the kids. I overheard an owl

talking. Fardels, step out front, will you, and tell
'em the kids aren't here."

With a heavy paw, the bear shoved Verity and
me behind him. Then he crawled outside and
stood up and, pretending to be grouchy, boomed,
"What's all this noise? Can't a bear sleep in the
morning? What boy? What girl?"

BA-LL-LL-OO-OO-OOOM!

A dark streak whistled down from the sky. It
slammed Fardels in his midsection, knocking him
over backwards into his cave. He sprawled on the
floor with a round thing squatting on his belly—
a glob of dripping muck the size of a bowling ball.

When Verity heard the bear hit the floor, she
scrambled over to him. "Fardels! Fardels, are you
all right?"

"Yeah," the bear grunted. "Just got the wind
knocked out of me." He sat up, brushing off slop.

Having seen the bombardment clearly—as my
sister hadn't—I wanted to crawl back into that
cave like a scared mole. I didn't want to look out
at the stone egg that hovered in the sky, talking
down to us.

LIE!	LIE!	LIE!
COME OUT!	OUT!	OUT!
OR DIE!	DIE!	DIE!

"I don't like this," said Lew. "They aren't just
whistling 'Dixie.' They've got a cannon. That first

little muck-pill was only a warning. The next one is going to flatten this cave."

I remembered the ball of mud that had crushed the farmhouse. Where the family named Weed-blossom didn't live any more.

"We'll go out and give ourselves up," said Verity briskly. "We don't want the owls to knock down Fardels's cave."

"All right," I quavered, after she'd twisted my arm a bit. "You go first."

"No, you don't," said the bear firmly. "Let 'em flatten the cave! You're staying here."

"I don't like this," said Lew Ladybug glumly. "They flatten this cave and they flatten the bunch of us, too."

All of a sudden a brilliant idea hit me. Hit me so hard I thought my head would burst.

"I've got it! I've got it! Listen! Why don't we all just take the back way out?"

The brown bear looked at me in honest puzzlement. "What back way?"

"Well, *our* bear cave on Earth has a back way," I insisted. "Why don't we take a look?"

The cave's rear wall was hidden by a mountain of fishheads and a load of dead leaves that the wind had driven in. My hopes toppled. I didn't think we could dig through it in less than a year.

Verity examined this garbage with her sniffer.

"Why, Fardels," she said in annoyance, "you have gone to the bathroom in here."

The bear shrugged. "It's a bear cave. What did you expect? Crocheted doilies?"

The owls' loudspeaker made a new demand.

COME OUT!	OUT!	OUT!
BY THE COUNT!	COUNT!	COUNT!
OF THREE!	THREE!	THREE!

The detective was dancing excitedly in the air. "For Pete's sake, Fardels, can't you move this trash out of the way and get that back door open?"

"I'll try. Come on, help me dig, Tim and Terrible Verity."

| **ONE!** | ONE! | ONE! |

It was a smelly job, but the owls' warning made us hop to it. Fardels hoisted armloads of fish-heads and flung them aside. I dropped to my knees and swatted the dead leaves madly, while Verity, wrinkling her nose, somewhat gingerly helped.

| **TWO!** | TWO! | TWO! |

"Timmy," said my sister, "I just had an awful thought. What if this bear cave isn't built like our New Jersey one? What if there isn't any back way out?"

"Keep digging," I suggested, digging harder myself.

Then Fardels whooshed aside a final armload, and there it was—a beautiful up-and-down crack in the rear wall.

THREE!   **THREE!**   THREE!

Verity and I jostled into the crack. Grunting, the bear followed.

BA-LL-OO-OOM! The cannon had spoken. Then from behind us came a closer *THA-RR-RR-RR-OO-OO-OOMMM!* The roof of the cave had fallen. Like a bunch of fleas blown by a puff from a bellows, we were picked up and flung, carried through the air on a swirling cloud of dust and pebbles and fishheads and torn-apart bundles of wood.

6. *"The Very Air Has Ears"*

Coughing and sneezing, our eyes burning from the dust, we found ourselves heaped at the bottom end of a narrow, downhill passageway. Luckily the bear had landed first, and his soft bulk had cushioned the rest of us. I picked myself up, only a little scraped. Lew was twittering comments about the owls, so I figured he was all right. As for Verity, she was laughing so hard you'd think she had just had a ride on a roller coaster.

The dust thinned, and I found myself looking out through a hole in a rock wall, easily wide enough to crawl out through, just like our bear cave on Earth. Beyond the hole I could see a patch of daylight. Grass-covered ground and bushes with green leaves.

On hands and knees, I crept out through the hole and emerged under a bush. Fresh air! I opened my dusty mouth and guzzled it. From

over my head came a loud mechanical roar. I parted the leaves and cautiously peered through.

What I saw just about froze me solid. Right over my bush, there hung this giant egg. It was a helicopter made of the owls' gray stone. It hung so low that the wind from its whacking propeller rumpled my hair. Behind its one round window sat an owl—the pilot, no doubt. I gulped and let the leaves rustle shut over me.

Had the owls seen me? Slowly and noisily, the stone egg circled overhead, making sure it had finished us off, while I stayed crouched down under my bush like a chicken afraid of a hawk. Satisfied at last that we were done for, the egg withdrew. The noise of its motor grew faint as it buzzed away.

Fardels and Lew and Verity crawled out after me and together we went around to the front of the hill to see what was left of the cave. All there was was a jumble of rocks with one corner of the FIREWOOD sign sticking out. On top of the ruins sat a dripping wet ball of muck as big as a house.

Fardels sighed. "*Now* where am I going to live?"

"Be glad you've still got that problem," Lew rasped.

"Yes, but *how* will I live? What'll I do—go around from door to door, dancing and begging for handouts? I can't live on nothing but honeycombs, you know. I'm a civilized bear. I like chocolate bars."

Verity made noises of sympathy, stroking the bear's brown fur.

"That's enough of that," said the bear gruffly, although I could see he didn't mind her attentions in the least.

I had a fresh brainstorm. "Fardels, why don't you come with me and Verity? We're going to go see this Raoul Owlstone and ask him to let loose of our grandparents. Why don't you talk with him too? Maybe he'll build you another cave."

A furious twittering sat down on my collar. "Kid," Lew exploded, "are you stark raving nuts? Can't you see this stone owl gang is merciless? Raoul Owlstone wouldn't even listen to you. He's so low that, even if he got up on stilts, he could walk under a gartersnake's bellybutton. Forget it. You go see him, baby, and you'll end up in the muck mine working a pick and shovel till you keel over."

"The bug is right," the bear said with a sigh.

"Then what'll we do?" I wanted to know.

"You'll stay out of trouble," Lew said evenly. "From now on"—he punched the air with a forefoot to stress his point—"I'm the one who's giving orders around here."

"Now look here, Lewis O. Ladybug," broke in Verity, all mad, "since when do we have to take orders from you? All you are is a tough-talking little bug no bigger than my fingernail. So if you think you're going to boss Timmy and me around like a crumby Grimble, you have another think coming."

"What are you getting sore at?" the detective snarled. "You're playing ball with me, angel, on account of your grandmother wants you to."

"Gran told you to stay with us?"

"Right. I've been retained. If you must know, your grandmother was mad at me. She said it was all my fault you kids followed me through the door. So I had to promise her I'd keep an eye on you. What else could I do? I take a case, I stick with it."

"All right, then," said Verity, "take us to our grandmother."

"Beautiful, be reasonable." The bug sighed. "Can't you guess what you're up against? You set one foot on Moonflower Mountain and—"

"Isn't it Mount Peeweehockey?" I interrupted, looking at the mountain on the skyline.

"Kid, you're not in New Jersey anymore. Like I say, just set one foot on that mountain—"

"Why would we want to?"

"Because that's where your grandfolks are. Only you'd better not go looking for them. You do, and a couple of thousand owls will swarm all over you."

I stared in curiosity at the far-off mountain. Wasn't it Mount Peeweehockey? I could barely see it for the dark oily clouds that hung around it—then for a moment the clouds parted, and on the mountain's nose I could make out a kind of wart, sort of toadstool-shaped. Besides, the mountain wore a black thing like a skullcap on its head.

The detective guessed my questions. "That mushroom-thing sitting out on that ledge—that's Owlstone Hall, Raoul's house, where his factory is. And that black hat on top of the mountain is solid glass. It's a dome, and Raoul stuck it over the Moonflower. Your grandmother is a prisoner under that dome, too."

"Then what are we waiting for?" Verity cried. "Let's get her out! And let's find Gramp, while we're at it! That's why we came to this crazy country. Timmy, why are you kicking me?"

"Just trying to shut you up," I said.

"NOW CUT THAT OUT!" said Lew, in a pretty loud voice for so small a person. "There isn't going to be any rescue. Haven't you two got me into enough hot water? You're not going to fight a whole owl army. I won't let you. A month from now, the full moon will come back and the door to Earth will reopen, and you can both go back to New Jersey again. Get me?"

"We get you, Lew," I said, keeping my fingers crossed.

Wearily, the detective turned to Fardels. "Bear, do you see what I'm up against? Keeping these kids in line is going to be tough. Especially the girl. I'll need help. Interested?"

And so the brown bear, having nothing better to do now that he'd lost his firewood business, took a job as Lew's assistant, and to pay him, Lew promised to help him hunt for honey and fish and blackberries. The two of them decided we would all set out for a nice quiet pond they knew about, where there'd be trout for the bear to catch. The owls wouldn't bother us there.

NOTE BY VERITY: *Were they ever wrong! But I'll let Timmy go on with the story.*

Fardels led the way, on all fours, his head and his hind end swaying from side to side. For anyone so big and clumsy-looking, he moved fast. It was all I could do to keep his stubby tail in sight. Verity, clinging to my shirt-tail, kept tripping over things. Seeing her difficulties, Lew ordered the bear to give her a ride on his back, and after that, we moved along at a more comfortable pace, following a trail thick with weeds, keeping underneath trees as much as we could, so as not to be seen from the sky. Every twenty minutes or so, Fardels would halt, and Verity would dismount, and the bear would scratch his back against a tree.

Around noon—it was hard to tell, because the sun always stayed behind clouds—we came to another river, a wide, important one. The way across it was over a wooden bridge. Leading up to the bridge ran a road of crushed pink shells that didn't look tire-tracked or oily. Cars, I figured, hadn't been invented in this country yet.

Just the same, the road was having a rush hour. That really handed me a surprise. People—a whole thick crowd of them—were flowing along that highway of unspoiled pink and over the bridge. The first Other Earth people I'd laid eyes on!

As soon as Lew had made sure that there were no owls in sight, we blended in with the moving crowd. Six or eight deep, all were trudging in the direction of Moonflower Mountain. We were to mingle with them till we were safely over the bridge, then we would drop back into the woods on the other side.

While we flowed along with the people, Lew on my collar kept saying, "No owls yet!" and "So far, so good!" while Fardels threw worried glances up to the sky.

You never saw a crowd more sad and dejected-looking. Most of the people kept their gaze fixed to the bridge and they walked as if they hoped they would never get where they were going. Some of them were staggering under big boxes and sacks that held, I guessed, all they had in the world. I trudged beside them, talking with them, and some told me that the owls had ordered them to leave their homes and go work in the mines. One guy was a mailman—he still wore a hat like a mailman on Earth, only with a bright purple flower in it. He was out of a job, he said, because there wouldn't be any letters any more. Raoul had decided that people didn't need to read or write, so he had done away with the mails, and with books and newspapers. Shuffling along beside me came a popcorn man. He was trundling a cart with a glass case that had once been filled with hot white stuff. Now it held his sweaters and socks. There was a woman who told me she had once sold balloons to children in parks, only now all the parks were kept locked. She too was off to the mines.

An old fellow in patched work jeans bustled up to me, a wicker basket swinging by its handle from one of his arms. From his upper lip, yellow moustaches stuck out like a couple of brushes for putting melted butter on raw piecrust with. "Want a tomato?" he asked, dipping a hand into his basket and holding out a ripe red thing as big as a fist.

"You bet!" I said.

"Thunderation!" said the farmer, watching me chomp away, "you eat like somebody hungry. You're good to see. Ain't you full of that fake muck like everybody else?"

"Muck?"

"Guess you ain't from around here, son. No, I can see by your clothes you ain't. Let me tell you, everybody's full of muck these days except you foreigners. Muck pills—the stone owls give 'em out. People eat 'em and get filled up, and they forget what real food tastes like. Nobody wants tomatoes any more. I can hardly give 'em away."

His moustaches quivered when he talked.

"I'll take one, please," said Verity from Fardels's back, as the brown bear fell into step along with us.

"Welcome to it, young lady," the farmer said. "Likely to be the last I'll ever raise. Can't grow a thing without sunshine." He glared at the cloud-choked sky.

All of us tramped along over the wooden boards, and while Verity and I lightened his basket, the old guy unloaded his mind. Once, he told us, the Land of the Moonflower had been ruled by a handful of wise old men and women called the Elders. "Not that they ever did much," the farmer explained, "because nothing much ever needed doing. The people were happy just to breathe out and in, and the Moonflower kept blooming all night and most all morning, and the air wasn't nothing but perfume. Then Raoul Owlstone came along. He met with the Elders and the next thing we knew, they declared that Raoul was the Dictator. Then Raoul, he clapped that glass dome over the Moonflower. Nobody could see it any more. Well sir, that was the worst thing he done, I'll tell you."

"You really miss the Moonflower, don't you?" said Verity sympathetically.

"Miss it? Why, child, the Moonflower was the center of everything. All the bugs and bees and windmill moths depended on its juice, and they'd fly around helping the crops to grow. People, too, needed that flower. When they were tired from work or worry they'd just look up at it there on the mountain, and they'd drink in the air and say, 'Ah! that makes me feel better!' So when Raouly Owly put that deadly dome over it, he took the heart right out of us. That dome was a terrible thing to build, too. I know. They made my brother work as a glassblower, blowing it."

We walked on in silence. Then the farmer said, "That's Owlstone Hall up there," and he pointed to the wart on the mountain's nose. "There's a factory in back of it for making owlstone. You know what owlstone is? It's gray foggy-looking stuff. The owls are made of it, and the flying eggs, and Owlstone Hall. Anyhow, that factory has smoked up everything. Makes me so mad I could—hello, Missus, want a tomato? Take your choice!"

This last was addressed to a woman who'd caught up with us. She wore a flowery dress and an apron and a worried look. She had one green eye and one brown. Anxiously, she wanted to know, "Has anyone seen my son? He's eleven, a little younger than you kids. Wildmustard Weedblossom, his name is. Have you heard anything of him?"

"I've heard of him," put in the farmer sourly. "The pesky brat, him and his model rocket ship that used to buzz circles around my barn. Scared my best milk cow so bad she dried up on me. Mustard Weedblossom—I'd like to catch him!"

Fardels growled, "The kid was only having fun," and I remembered that this Mustard—if it was the same kid—had painted the brown bear's firewood sign.

"Didn't you live in that house with the red shutters?" I asked the woman. "The house that got crushed by a muck bomb?"

"Ours wasn't the only one," she said sadly. "The owls have been muck-bombing everybody. They want all the people to leave home and go work in Raoul's mine."

"What's become of your husband?" asked Lew. "He's Doc Weedblossom, the inventor, right?"

The woman's different-colored eyes grew moist. "If only I knew where he is! But I've lost him too. You see, as soon as Raoul became Dictator the owls arrested my husband and they flew away with him. I was practically out of my mind. Wild-mustard wanted to rescue his father. I begged the boy not to try, but he headed for Owlstone Hall. That was weeks ago. I—I don't know what's happened to either of them."

Bombed out of her house, Mrs. Weedblossom, too, was headed for the mountain. She hoped Owlstone Hall could use a waitress. If she got such a job, she might hear news of her husband and her son. I liked her a lot, and I hoped she would have some luck, and then she hugged Verity and me and hurried on, pleading for news from the other people.

"Sometimes," the popcorn man said slowly, "I wonder if Raoul Owlstone is doing right."

"Doing right?" shrilled the farmer. "Why, ungum your eyes and ears, you dad-burned butterslinger! Doing right? Why, bless you, Raoul is doing as wrong as ever he can. Look up at that mountain with that ugly glass dome on it. Look at that old Owlstone Hall of Raoul's, like a toadstool on the mountain's nose. Don't you remember when you could look up and see that mountain all covered with blossoms and shiny vines? Remember them windmill moths streaming up and down, like a river o' rainbows? It ain't Moonflower Mountain no more. They ought to call it Blacktop Bump. What's the matter with the Elders, anyhow? They must be fast asleep. Raoul Owlstone has turned this country all around, and the whole thing's a durned sight worse."

"Careful," the popcorn man said worriedly, "don't let the owls hear you. They've got listening devices, you know. The very air has ears."

"Plague take them and their devices!" bawled the farmer, growing madder all the time. "Who ever saw a stone owl in the daytime, anyway? Night's when they fly. They're like bats. Oh, I know, they go a-sneaking round the country in their flying eggs, listening in on folks, but what are you worrying for? There's nary an egg in the sky."

"LOOK OUT!" shouted Lew, whose compound eyes had been keeping watch. To Fardels he yelled, "Dive off, bear!"

Without a murmur the brown bear leaped to his hind feet, dumping off Verity, strode to the side of the bridge and straddled a railing. He took a deep breath and, feet first, let himself go.

He dropped like a furry brown bomb until he splashed into the water. It must have been seventy feet down to the river below.

Why had Lew given this order? All of a sudden a stone egg swooped down from the sky, its huge propeller whacking right over our heads. From under it a long thick tube came curling. As I watched in horror, the tomato farmer was snatched right up. He went whooshing into the tube like a mouse caught by a vacuum cleaner. A sucking noise—*shloof!*—and then another, and the popcorn man also disappeared.

For a couple of minutes the stone egg hung in the air above us, snarling as if to say, "Does anyone else want to speak?" And then, as suddenly as it came, it shot straight into the sky and churned away. The people on the bridge fixed their eyes on the planks under their feet and went back to trudging the road.

7. *The Rising of the Pond*

Slowly and soggily, his fur all pasted flat, Fardels hauled himself up onto the riverbank. The rest of us, having crossed the bridge, had dropped out of the mournful parade.

"Bear," said Lew, "you look like a drowned sofa. Hey, stop! Don't shake the whole river on us!"

"You got me into it, boss," the wet bear growled.

The detective glowered. "Well, you *had* to take that dive. What if the owls had seen you and these kids together? The owls are rock-heads, all right, but maybe they would have wised up. Now they'll still think their bomb finished us off. OK, let's move."

With Verity once more on top of the bear's back, we set off along a path through a thick pine forest. It was hot. All around my head, gnats kept doing dances. We kept heading in a zigzagging beeline toward Moonflower Mountain. The weak sun hung low in the sky when at last we reached our destination—a little bright pond in the shape of an oval, not twenty yards wide. A sign on one of its shores gave its name. CRESSIDA POND.

Right away Verity declared she was hot and dusty, and she was going for a swim.

"Now, Sis," I said uneasily, "you don't know how deep this pond is. What if it's crawling with snapping turtles?"

Wrinkling her nose at me, Verity kicked off her sneakers and strode into the pond, shirt and pants and all. I watched her swimming around having a fine time, and after a long debate with my fears, I jumped in too.

Cressida Pond was warm, its water clearer than glass. You could just barely touch your toes to the bottom. On my back, lazily floating, I watched a windmill moth go twirling by. A rainbow trout jumped for the moth, missed it, splashed down again. In the birch trees circling the shore I could see Lew Ladybug hunting for aphids and the brown bear searching for honey-trees. Suddenly all that had troubled me packed up and vanished—my worries about finding Gran and Gramp, about Mrs. Weedblossom and her lost husband and son, about the farmer and the popcorn man. For the moment, I was as happy as a little kid in a tub, and not in any hurry to get lathered.

After our cooling swim, Verity and I felt like doing something to thank the pond, so she took a stick and raked dead leaves away from the shore and I relieved the water of a rotten picnic basket.

Lew made a landing on my collar. "Not one single aphid," he said. "Nothing but runt-sized mealybugs."

Fardels joined us, cupping a group of blackberries in one paw. "All I could find," he said gruffly. "You kids have 'em." But Verity made him take a share of them, too.

Luckily, watercress grew at the edge of the pond, so I bundled up an armload of the crisp green stuff and the three of us mammals had supper, sort of a vegetable one. Then Lew tried working his magnifying-glass wings on some charcoal that a picnicker had forgotten. Perched on a charcoal pellet, he brought a few weak sunbeams to a point, and after a while he got a fire smoldering. Verity and I huddled next to it, and soon our clothes felt less soggy.

As we sprawled in the grass I asked, "Lew, what's it like to be a ladybug?"

"It's the cream, kid—that is, it used to be. Back before Owly threw a dome over the Moonflower. When I had my office on the Moonflower I used to spend my days picking big, sweet aphids off of that swell plant. Runny and warm they were, like your breakfast soft-boiled egg. After I'd had my fill, I'd pick out a blossom and crawl in between its petals, find me a warm spot, and just dream till the moon came out. Then I'd watch the Moonflower open. Kid, until you've watched the Moonflower open, you haven't seen anything. There isn't anything more beautiful in this world."

Birds were singing their last numbers for the day, and now the sky looked shadowy. Fardels Bear was sloshing around up to his belly in the pond. "Got you!" he shouted, making a catch. A plump trout wriggled between his paws.

Just as the bear was lifting the fish head-first to his jaws, it happened. Something strange and beautiful and—well, I can hardly believe it even now.

From the center of the pond rose a woman's head. She had flowing hair, and twined in it, she was wearing a huge white water lily. But she wasn't an ordinary person. Her hair was slightly green, and, the strangest thing of all, you could see right through her. Her eyes and nose and hair and everything were made of water. That's right. Water. It was as if she'd been carved out of ice and had melted, keeping her shape.

The water woman frowned. Her lips moved, and when words came out, they sounded tinkling and far away, as though they had bubbled up from several fathoms.

"*Let go of her! Let go of Fiona!*"

The rainbow trout spurted from between the brown bear's paws, creased the surface of the pond, and wriggled away. Thunderstruck, Fardels stumbled backwards out of the water.

"Excuse me, lady," he stammered, "I—I thought—"

"You thought you would sup on my fish," the liquid voice finished for him. "Well, you won't. You're welcome to drink from me and to pick my watercress, but the fish are under my protection. Is that clear?"

The bear nodded, shuffling from foot to foot like a kid caught stealing apples.

Then the transparent face turned to Verity and me and gave us a beautiful smile. "Thank you. That was kind of you to rake my shore and take that trash away."

"Who—who are you?" Verity wanted to know.

"I'm Cressida Pond, of course. Who did you think I was?"

"You're *alive*? And we went swimming in you?"

Cressida Pond tossed back her head and laughed a long, tinkling laugh that sounded like one hundred gallons of water falling down a flight of stairs. "People swim in me all the time. That is, they used to. Lately there haven't been many picnickers. In fact, until you came along, I was feeling neglected. Would you like to meet my fish? They're Finn and Fiona MacCool. If you like, they'll put on a show for you."

"Oh yes, please!" said Verity and I, almost together.

The two rainbow trout leaped into the air and made a kind of bow. For the next ten minutes we were treated to the most unusual water show ever. The fish kept doing back flips and jackknife dives, bursting up from below and spouting like fountains and letting the water woman juggle them in her hands. I kept up a running account of the show for Verity, and when it was done we clapped, and the bear clapped the loudest of anybody.

Cressida Pond wanted to know what was the matter with the country. A windmill moth seldom went by. Nothing seemed to multiply, except muckhawks. "And look at my white birch trees! Their bark is turning gray! What has gone wrong with the world?"

"What's wrong, ma'am," said Lew, "is Raoul Owlstone. He's built a dome over the Moonflower so that nobody can see it, and the moths can't drink its juice. All the trees and plants are croaking right and left because Raoul's factory smokes so bad it blots out the sun. You see, ma'am, Raoul loves muck and murk. For him they're a whole way of life."

The surface of the pond quivered with her rage. "The nerve of him! To hide the Moonflower from its country! What's to be done about this polluter, this outlaw, this—?"

The detective shrugged. "I wish I could tell you. What makes things tough is that he's got an army of owls."

"Maybe," Verity put in, "the answer is just to talk with him. To tell him he isn't treating the country right. Maybe Timmy and I will see him. We want to ask him to let go of Gran and Gramp."

The detective blew up. "Stow it, baby! For the last time, I'm telling you it would never work. It wouldn't do any good to talk to Raoul Owlstone. He wouldn't listen. You're not going to see Raoul Owlstone, you're not going anywhere near Raoul Owlstone. Now will you behave yourself and knock that goofy notion out of your head?"

"Sure, sure, Lew," I tried to calm him, "whatever you say."

Verity, disgusted with me, threw a punch at my ribs that missed. But Cressida Pond's clear face wore a knowing smile.

"Timothy Tibb," she said to me, "I can see through you as easily as you see through me. You're frightened, you don't trust yourself, but there's courage at the bottom of you. It's a good thing you have this ladybug to advise you. And Verity, you too need an adviser and a friend. I have a gift for you. Here, take this!"

A transparent hand had reached in under a lily pad and was offering something to Verity. The gift was little, round, and yellowed like ancient ivory.

"Always keep it with you," said the water woman. "Its name is Percy-Mary Bysshe-Wollstonecraft Shelley Snail."

In Verity's right palm, the snail opened a tiny mouth underneath it, and spoke in a high, shrill voice with a pause after each word:

"Call. Me. Shelley. For. Short."

"Oh, thank you, Cressida Pond," said my sister excitedly. "You're so lovely—if only I could see you! Be my good luck charm, Shelley Snail. All right if I carry you in my back pocket?"

"That. Ought. To. Be. A. Quiet. Place. I. Guess. —My. Favorite. Food. Is. Mildewed. Watercress."

Lew snorted. "Takes this joker a week just to get a sentence out."

"Patience, ladybug," said Cressida gently. "You'll find the snail well worth listening to. It is a poet and a prophet. It can tell you what tomorrow holds in store."

"Shelley, can you actually do that?" Verity wondered.

The snail's pinpoint eyes wobbled on little stalks. It spoke again, in verse:

I. Draw. Into. My. Shell. And. There. I. Hear.
The. Ocean. Of. The. Future. Rushing. Near.
I. See. Its. Breakers. Stumble. In. And. Bow.—
My. Shell. Is. Small. —I. Can't. See. Far. From.
  Now.

"OK, then, snail, how about a short-range prediction?" Lew demanded. "It's getting dark. Where are we going to spend the night?"

The snail's horned head drew back into its shell. After what seemed forever, it reappeared.

You'll. Climb. A. Hill. A. Stone's. Throw. From. This. Beach.
On. Whose. Crest. Grows. A. Celebrated. Peach.

Fardels wrinkled his brow, working at thinking. "Could the snail mean—? I know! Old Man Clingstone's place! Nobody's peaches are more famous. His orchard's right over there on top of that next hill."

"Yeah," Lew said grudgingly, "yeah, it makes sense. I was thinking of that very hill myself. We'd be on high ground. We could watch out for anything coming."

"Then be off with you before darkness falls," said Cressida. She waved a slender arm. Her smile took us all in, even the forgiven Fardels.

A path climbed upward. We tramped our way up the side of the hill, me with Lew on my collar. I glanced behind me to see Cressida's face and flowing hair slowly dissolve to a level surface of water.

I felt glad that she had given the snail to Verity, not to me. I would have felt sort of strange carrying a poet and prophet around in my back pocket.

8. *The Snail Foretells*

The full moon, bales of cloud in front of it, had a hard job trying to shine. Standing close to the first peach tree in the orchard, I could just barely make out a sign, hand-lettered by some terrible speller:

Gon 2 work
in the mine

FREE PEECHES

Help Yorself

Sure I would. Hungrily, I twisted a big peach loose from the nearest branch and bit into it. The fruit was so hard and green I almost fractured my teeth.

"Save your appetite, Tim," said the detective. "Those fuzz-balls used to be famous, but now they aren't getting ripe any more."

In spite of my disappointment with the peaches, I was happy to get to the orchard on top of the hill. Its trees clustered around us like good buddies. At least we'd be able to get our sleep tonight.

Or would we? Fardels was patrolling the hillside. All of a sudden he rose on his hind legs and sniffed the air. "Something's coming," he growled. "Hear it?"

I listened. A low rumbling sound crept uphill out of the pines—a steady boom, like faraway traffic.

"Stay here, bear," Lew told him. Don't go down there—a big bozo like you is too noticeable. I'll fly down myself and take a look-see." He darted off.

Beneath us the tops of the pine trees stretched to the edge of the sky. From the hilltop it was like looking down on a campground pitched with a thousand dark green tents. Moonflower Mountain stood on the skyline, its nose hidden in clouds. Near the foot of our hill, Cressida Pond slept inside her circle of white birches, her waters calm under the faint moon, but dancing with pinpoints of light.

The rumbling drew closer. Now a river of shadow was flowing out of the woods, steadily creeping uphill. Shapes with round heads were bobbling along in it.

Lew was back on my collar. "Bad luck," he rasped. "It's owls. Hundreds of 'em. That noise is their ball-bearings rolling on the ground. I picked up some of their radio chatter. A muck-hawk saw you kids down by the pond."

A chill shot to my toes as if an ice cube had slithered down my back. "Lew, let's run! Come on—"

"Use your head, sweetpuss," the detective cut in, snarling. "They've got this hill surrounded. Anyhow, you can't outrun a rolling owl."

"Lew, what'll we do, Lew?"

"Shut up while I think."

Verity was drumming her fists against a tree trunk the way you'd beat on a bolted door. "Why?" she was wailing, "why did I have to lose my glasses? If only I could see, even a little bit—"

With an effort I gulped down my own fear. "Sis, you *can* help. Dig out that snail of yours, will you? Ask it how we're going to get out of here."

"Oh, skunk cabbage," said the bear. "By the time the snail answers, the owls will be all over us."

But my sister, remembering the water woman's gift, quit howling. She drew the little yellow shell out of her pocket and started talking to it.

Mixed with the far-off rumble was a new sound now, like that of a great weight jolting along. The ladybug had heard it. Perched on the back of my hand, he broke out his rear wings and placed one on top of the other.

"Look through me, kid," he barked at me. "Take a squint down there and tell me what you see."

NOTE BY VERITY: *That was one of Lew's features. He could make himself into either a magnifying glass or a telescope, depending on how he arranged his wings.*

Through the simple telescope of the detective, I studied the land below. At the bottom of the hill six owls were dragging a sort of log made out of owlstone, that rolled on two owlstone wheels. They got it where they wanted it and aimed it up the hill.

"It's a cannon," I said, keeping my voice steady. But my nerves were jingling like dimes in a jelly jar.

Lew flicked himself shut. "Rats," he commented.

"Don't worry, boss," said the bear. "I'll make trouble for them."

"Yeah," the detective grunted, "but for how long? Verity, for Pete's sake, hasn't your snail come out yet?"

BOOM!

A *whoosh* in the air over our heads and down sailed a mudpie as big as a bathtub. It crash-landed in the top branches of the tree we stood under. Twigs and blobs of muck showered on us.

Lew gave a whistle. "That one was high. Next time they'll aim for your ankles."

A column of owls, two abreast, had rolled half-way up our hillside. Now they kept on climbing, their electric eye-cells gleaming through the dark. Beside me, Verity talked worriedly into her cupped hand, trying to get the snail to answer her. I was starting to fall to pieces with the shakes.

Then an extra-tall owl out in front of the rest waved a wing and the column halted. The tall one was so close I could watch its beak flap as it talked. "Bear—Boy—Girl! You are up there in the orchard. Surrender!"

"Keep quiet," Lew shot to us. "Don't answer it. You'd only improve their aim."

"This is your last warning," the machine-voice droned. "Surrender. Surrender or we will come up after you."

"Just you try, you rotten rock-hunk," the brown bear said under his breath.

Another *BOOM!* and a second bathtub of mud dropped in front of us. This time, to my amazement, Fardels stepped forward and caught it in his arms. Staggering under its weight, he lifted it high and with a terrible roar flung it back downhill into the column of owls.

And do you know what?—his aim was perfect. The owl commander caught the muck-bomb right in the beak, keeled over backwards, and lay under it.

Loud cheers rang out on our hilltop. They were coming out of *me*.

Their leader fallen, the rest of the stone owls turned around in confusion and rolled back down to the bottom of the hill. But their cannon hadn't quit.

BOOM!

BOOM-A-LOOM!

BA-LOOM!

Fresh tub-sized hunks of muck kept splattering down on us. Faithfully, the bear would catch every one and toss it back. He did fine for a while, but soon I could see he was tiring.

"Can't keep this up much longer, boss," he said between his teeth. "Must be some easier way to fight owls. Why don't I just go smash 'em?"

"Hold on," Lew said sharply, "you can't fight a whole army."

This excitement was too much for me. My legs collapsed and lowered me to the ground.

Verity was waving a hand with a poet-and-prophet in it. "Quiet, everybody! Shelley is going to utter!"

The snail's head had poked out of its shell, horns twitching. We listened as it piped:

Stone. Legions. Fall. Before. A. Raging. Beast—
Beware. The. Smells. Of. An. Engaging. Feast.

"Horsefeathers!" sputtered the bear. "Who's a raging beast?"

"Fardels, it means you," I told him. "Stone legions—that's the owls—will fall before you! Hooray!"

"But what's this stuff about a feast?" put in Lew. "Makes no sense to me."

Verity frowned in puzzlement. "Shelley, don't be so mysterious. Will you please explain yourself?"

"I. Just. Make. The. Prophecies," said the snail word by word. "I. Don't. Make. Sense. Of. Them."

I kept turning the prophecy over and over in my mind, picking at it the way you'd pick at a tough knot. *The smells of a feast.* But then I didn't have any more time to ponder, because the enemy had rallied. Now they were flowing back up the slope again in a column six owls wide, a new tall owl commander rolling in front of them.

The sight threw Fardels into a rage. He didn't wait for any orders from Lew. His huge head bent, his paws swatting left and right, he went charging downhill straight for the oncoming column. Owls fell, then bobbed back up again—their rounded bottoms made them hard to knock over for keeps—but the bear just kept on swatting. He was a whirlwind of fur. Sometimes he'd take two owls and slam their heads together and stun their mechanical brains. Then they'd roll back down the hillside looking absentminded. Sometimes he'd toss owls to either side of him. He kept on charging downhill through the middle of the column, dividing it the way a comb makes a part. Before long the whole hillside was strewn with gray stone, like the columns of some knocked-over temple.

At last, after they'd lost yet another commander, the owls retreated once more down into the shadows. All this time, I had been giving Verity a blow-by-blow account of the fight. When Fardels, panting and tired, rejoined us, Verity hugged him hard.

A merrier get-together you never did see. The brown bear pranced around on his hind legs, growling what he thought was a song. Verity danced around him in a circle. The snail had been right! A raging beast had beaten a legion of owls! I felt pretty cocky. With Fardels to fight, Lew to scout and direct us, and Shelley to foretell the future, how could we lose? What dictator could beat us now?

Lew had guessed my thoughts. "Don't be smug, kid. We were just lucky this time, that's all."

A cold gray dawn was breaking. At least, the oily sky was growing somewhat light. And then— had I gone crazy? Floating down out of the air came wonderful breakfast aromas.

Bacon...

Scrambled eggs...

Buckwheat pancakes with honey...

Oatmeal with brown sugar and plenty of cream...

Hot blueberry muffins with butter on them,

and the sharp tang of lemon marmalade...

It was too much for me. I was starving. With Verity right beside me, I bounded out from under the peach trees and followed my twitching nose.

Fardels was on his feet and moving. "What's that I smell? Fresh brook trout?"

"It's a trap, you ninnies!" the detective shrieked from my collar. "Don't you understand? The owls, they've lured you out of the orchard! The smells of a feast—that's just what the snail said to watch out for, right?"

Dumbfounded, we stood under open sky on the hillside. And then a stone egg—which had broadcast those artificial odors—swooped low and hung right over our heads. Its vacuum-cleaner tube came squirming downward, like the tube that had caught the tomato farmer and the popcorn man.

"Look out, bear!" cried Lew—too late.

A sickening *SHLUPPP!*—and Fardels, kicking all four legs, shot up into the nozzle and was gone.

Another *SHLUPP!* Up and away went Verity. I watched the soles of her sneakers wigwag and disappear.

I was rooted, too terrified to run. A rush of air hoisted me up off the ground. Now I was shooting straight up into the swallowing tube—
SHLUPPPP!

9. Between the Worst Two Beaks

Rouser was barking. The muck-cannon was booming. Bacon and pancakes and muffins came snowing down out of the air. Now I was sitting on a lily pad in the middle of Cressida Pond, cracking a soft-boiled egg. Bits of shell crumbled, and inside the egg was Peepy Treetoad. He snickered, "I saw you shove that owl into that river," and I hollered and flung him away. Now I was squatting on my three-legged chair in the kitchen of Grimbles' farmhouse. A label was sticking to my tongue. Maw Grimble was coming toward me, lifting her masher—no, all of a sudden it wasn't a masher, it was a miniature Moonflower.

I was having nightmares. When the nozzle had whooshed me up, I must have blacked out. Next thing I knew, I was coming to my senses inside the owlstone helicopter, lying face down on its vibrating deck, listening to its propeller's steady *whack—whack—whack—*

Slowly, my eyes got used to the gloomy light. I could make out an owl pilot sitting at a control panel. On the deck beside me, Verity was rubbing her eyes, and nearby, ringed by more owls, Fardels Bear lay on his back, growling quietly. But where was Lew? For a moment I thought I had lost him. Then a twitter under my left ear told me that he had only changed collar lapels.

"Well, kids," he said dryly, "it looks like you're going to get your wish. They're taking you to see him—Raoul Owlstone—the big cheese himself!"

At last! We would meet the mysterious Dictator! Once I had thought I wanted to. Now I wasn't so sure.

I stared out over the owl pilot's head through a round porthole. Beneath us, black treetops were racing by. The pit of my stomach was falling like an elevator. I'd never been up in any kind of aircraft before. High places always scared me. And then the mountain that looked like Peewee-hockey filled the whole porthole, its black glass skullcap giving off faint light. The giant dome, I remembered, held my grandmother a prisoner—and the Moonflower, whatever *that* was.

Circling the mountain now, our stone egg suddenly plunged into a dirty snowbank of cloud, while my stomach tried to climb me like a ladder. Fog swirled around us—thickened—thinned—and the nose of the mountain appeared, wearing its round, gray blob.

"Last stop," barked Lew, "Owlstone Hall!"

Scared though I was, I was fascinated. A co-lossal toadstool, that's just what the house looked like. It was completely made of gray owlstone—just a round, bulging roof on top of a thick stem. Instead of windows it had narrow slits for peering from. One lonesome smokestack rose from the toadstool's crown. Thick smoke poured out of it—from the factory that made the owls, no doubt. Two more stone eggs like ours went swooping by, circling the Hall, guarding it. On the edge of the roof sat a muckhawk gobbling a songbird. A bright green feather dropped.

Soon, with a jolt, our egg bumped down onto the rooftop. A slab of its wall fell out and became a gangplank, which the owls urged us to walk. Four owls took charge of Fardels. Verity and I rated only an owl apiece.

Inside the Hall, we were hurried down an owlstone stairway and along an owlstone corridor, then we were prodded into a tremendous owlstone room. It was the biggest room I'd ever seen, and so dim I could barely see to its opposite side. And *cold*? Like a North Pole cave. A cave the size of twenty-four basketball courts.

NOTE BY VERITY: *People*—reliable *people*—*tell me the room was no bigger than twenty basketball courts. If that many.*

By the light of guttering candles, I made out a woman and a man. They were sitting face to

face at the two ends of a table a hundred feet
long. At first I thought the man was made out of
owlstone like everything else. He was big and
round. From across the room, one of his shoulders looked higher than the other, but as we hiked
and hiked and finally neared him, I could see
that a large brown-spotted bird —a muckhawk—
was using him for a perch. The man had his nose
sunk into a plate as big around as the lid of a
trash can. He was tearing into a stack of pancakes.
Buttery steam blew my way and reminded me
that I hadn't had any breakfast, only the smell of
it. Silent owls in gold-roped uniforms kept rolling
up to the table, forking more pancakes onto the
big man's plate.

The woman, too, was breakfasting, from a dish
as small as a doll's. If she was on a diet she didn't
need to be, because already she looked as skinny
as a skeleton. Her face and her hands were chalk
white. Her reddish hair was screwed tightly into
a bun. Her nose was a sharp white beak with little
red-berry warts on it, and she had on a long white
dress with a cape the color of fresh blood.
Clenched in her right eye was a rose-red monocle.
Her teeth were ratty and sharp, and her face wore
a sneer that seemed printed there. Together, that
man and that woman were a couple of real mean
birds, let me tell you. Like an overstuffed gray
owl and a bony red-and-white buzzard.

"That dame," Lew whispered to me, "calls herself the Baroness Ratisha von Bad Radisch. She's poison, junior. Keep your lip buttoned."

When we arrived at his end of the table, the master of Owlstone Hall raised a beaklike nose and, glaring, looked us over. He could have passed for a stone owl himself. His eyes stared out from dark gray circles. His pointed ears seemed hairy, or feathery. He wore a gray, moth-eaten sweater that a bowl of oatmeal must have spilled on long ago. He scowled at us and chewed, not saying anything.

The Baroness Ratisha quit picking at her bird-seed, or whatever it was, and fixed a beady eye on us through her rose-red monocle. "So here they are!" she sneered, "the ones who defeated the Army of Owlstonia! Two little kids and a bear! Raoul, your owls must be slipping!" She had to shout to her breakfast companion, the table being so long.

"As a rule," said the Dictator in a deep, hooting voice, "I don't see troublemakers. But I wanted a look at you. You knocked over forty-seven of my owls. There are only three of you?"

I quaked in my shoes, keeping my lip buttoned, but Verity spoke right up. "Five of us, Mister Dictator, counting Lew Ladybug and Shelley Snail. Turn on the lights, will you please? I can't see a thing in here."

Raoul gave a low, mocking laugh. "Oh, you won't be in the dark for long. What'll we do with them, Chuckles?"

This question went to the muckhawk on his shoulder. The bird opened its beak and let out a scream: *"Meat! Eat meat!"*

The Dictator peered at me with narrowed owl-eyes. "You, boy, are you the one that pushed the patrol owl into the river?"

"Tell him it was somebody else," Lew advised me.

"It—it couldn't have been *me*," I quavered.

"Certainly, it could have," butted in Verity, mad at my fib. "Timmy did it, and I'm proud of him."

The Dictator chuckled unpleasantly. "Let's call another witness. I happen to have one on me."

A hand fished into the pocket of his filthy sweater and pulled out something little and green and squirming. Peepy Treetoad, the spy who'd wanted Verity and me to collect June bugs for him.

"Look 'em over, Toad," Raoul commanded. "Ever see these kids before?"

Up from the palm of Raoul's pudgy hand, the toad blinked at us with glee. "That's them," he chirped.

Fardels growled and took a stride forward, but the owls closed in on him. From my collar, Lew burst out in angry twitters: "Cheap stinker! Judas toad! You'd sell your own mother for a June bug! Toad stool-pigeon!"

Raoul was watching me as if he was getting ready to swoop down on a mouse.

"Say," piped up the toad, "what about my reward, Your Excellency? A thousand June bugs you promised me, isn't that right?"

Raoul leered.

"Er—five hundred, maybe?" suggested the toad, coming down in price.

Raoul just chuckled.

"Well now," said the spy, looking worried, "fifty June bugs would be plenty. That would be very generous of Your Excellency."

"Worthless toad," said Raoul, "why should I pay you anything? Chuckles, baby! Here's a snack for you!"

The tree toad let out a squeak as Raoul's fat hand raised him to the muckhawk's beak. I hate to tell you this, but the bird, in finishing off Peepy, had to take four bites. At last Raoul lowered his empty hand and wiped it on the tablecloth. Then he smeared jam on a shingle of toast and pigged it down. Somehow, I didn't feel hungry any more.

My sister had heard the toad's last moments. "Raoul Owlstone," she said, almost in tears, "I think you're perfectly horrible."

Raoul was pointing at Fardels. "That bear. Isn't it the brown bear from the zoo, the one that escaped? Speak up, bear, is it you?"

"It's me," growled Fardels. "And I want to know what you've done with the other zoo animals. Where's my friend Boswell Boa Constrictor?"

Raoul hooted a laugh. "I—ho! ho!—threw 'em into the meat locker. Had a lot of 'em ground up for sausage. Why, this happens to be your buddy I'm eating now. I like a little snake meat with my pancakes."

And he forked up a sausage and waved it, steaming, under the brown bear's nose. "Want a bite?" the Dictator jeered. "You *used* to be fond of him, eh?"

The brown bear arched his back and bared his incisors. I expected he'd throw himself straight at Raoul. The muckhawk on the Dictator's shoulder fluttered nervously. But more owls quickly rolled in between their master and Fardels.

"Have a care, bear," Raoul taunted. "I could run you, too, through the grinder." He lifted the sausage to the muckhawk. The bird gaped its beak. The sausage vanished. The empty fork came down. The bird chomped hungrily.

Fardels looked ready to cry. "Boswell. You did that to Boswell. Boswell was the finest snake I know."

The Dictator scowled. "I've tasted better."

"Oh, la-de-da," said the baroness impatiently, drumming the tabletop with her sharp red nails. "Spare us the sermons, bear. Raoul, dear," she called down the long table, "haven't we had enough animals and children for one morning? They bore me dreadfully."

"Hold on, Ratisha," the Dictator shot back. "I want to question them. Speak up, boy, what are you doing here on Other Earth?"

I mustered all the bravery I had. "Mister Dictator," I began in a voice that shook, "we came here because you've got hold of our grandparents, Agamemnon and Agatha Duff of Morris Plains, New Jersey, and we want you to let them come home with us."

"And another thing," Verity put in hotly, "when are you going to lift that awful glass dome from over the Moonflower? It's hurting all the bees and the windmill moths. In fact, everything in this country is dying. Why don't you stop all the muck and smoke? Why don't you tell your owls to start being kind to animals? Bears, especially."

The Baroness Ratisha was staring through her eyepiece at my sister the way you'd look at your toothbrush if you had found a caterpillar on the end of it. "What sentimental parp," she said.

The Dictator scowled more darkly. "You think *your* grandparents are the only ones? Why, girl, I've got lots of people's grandparents down in the mine. As for the Moonflower, I'd like to burn it, chop it, root it out. So. You don't like the way I'm running this country? Do you think *you*, a blind kid like you, could do better?"

·

Verity thought. "I guess I could," she said slowly, "if someone showed me how."

"*Eat! Eat meat!*" the muckhawk screamed.

The baroness flashed white rat-teeth. "Raoul, these urchins are insulting you. Why waste your time on them? Can't we get on with breakfast?"

"How can I get on with it?" shot back Raoul. "Why, there isn't a pancake on my plate! Waiter, some food! Are you trying to starve me? OK, now, bear, tell me, how did you destroy all those owls? My valuable owls, made in my image? Talk fast, or it's the sausage grinder."

"Ahhhh," said Fardels in disgust, "your owls are pushovers."

Raoul's fork, with a new pancake on it, hung in midair. "Pushovers, did you say? My owls?"

"That's right," said the brown bear, "they're as easy as kicking over toadstools. Want me to show you what I did to them?"

Raoul nodded, interested.

Two owls stood between the bear and the Dictator. Quick as a shaggy lightning bolt, Fardels lashed out with his front paws, slamming the owls in their chests. Off balance, the pair crashed over, their ball-bearings spinning. They hit the floor. They lay still.

The Dictator's jaw sagged. The fork with its untasted pancake slowly settled to the table.

"My owls," Raoul said wonderingly. "I didn't

know anybody could do that to my owls."

At his command, two fresh owls rolled in and cleared away the wreckage of their companions. Four more owls surrounded Fardels, two on each side.

The baroness was trembling with fury. "You fool, Raoul, are you going to sit there stuffing your face while this hairy brute destroys your whole army?"

The Dictator flung her a snarl. "Hold your tongue, Ratty, or I'll have it held for you. All right, bear, that was a lucky trick. Got any more?"

"If you really want to know," said Fardels, "sometimes I did *this*—"

Turning to the owls on his left, he collected the pair in his arms and bashed their heads together. *THUNK!* The owls dropped to the floor, their transitors—or something—broken. An instant later the brown bear did the same to the pair on his right side, too. The air was choking with the thick black dust of cracked-open batteries.

For a long while Raoul and Ratisha sat there looking at each other. A thick blanket of dust had settled over Raoul's pancakes.

"Nincompoop!" the baroness shrieked at last, dabbing dust from her rose-red monocle. "Honestly, Raoul, at times I suspect you of stupidity. Ugh—this dust! I insist you put that bear through the sausage grinder!"

Her idea didn't set well with Fardels. A low

roar rumbled out of him. On his hind legs, paws
extended, he made straight for the baroness.

But the skinny witch just froze. In her right
eye, the pink eyepiece flashed, and she murmured, "Watch, bear, just watch. Look at the
lovely red light."

The monocle started to spin. Around and
around it went, faster and faster, brighter and
brighter. I had to tear my eyes away from it, it
was so fascinating.

"Now, bear," the baroness said oozily, "you will
do as I say. Lie down!"

Like a good dog, the brown bear slumped at
her feet. He had been hypnotized! The monocle
stopped its spin, a gleam of triumph in it.

"Ratty," said the Dictator with a chuckle, "I'll
have to hand it to you. Your eyeglass puts 'em
under, every time."

He clapped his hands. In rolled a dozen more
owls—this time, extra-tall ones. He was opening
his mouth to give more orders and get rid of us
when Lew chirped, "Wait! Hold on!"

And the loyal detective skimmed from my collar to the tablecloth and marched straight on up
to Raoul like a knight in spotted armor. Drawing
himself to his full height—an eighth of an inch—
he threw down his words with studied careless-
ness.

"Listen, Raoul Owlstone, you don't have any
say over these kids. They aren't even citizens of

this country. Let them go in my custody—I'm a licensed private investigator—and I'll see that they leave Other Earth on the next full moon."

For answer, Raoul just puffed his cheeks and blew a gust of air that swirled Lew up off the table. The ladybug fell back down, underbelly up, feet waving. After a few tries, rocking back and forth, he got his third pair of legs to touch the tablecloth, and righted himself.

"Let those kids go?" jeered the Dictator. "Nothing doing, bug. They'll never leave Owlstone Hall. Do you think I want them running around telling people that my owls are breakable? Anyhow, this is MY country and I'll do what I like. I'm the Dictator here, and that puts me above the law. All you are is a puny ladybug."

Lew glared at Raoul with contempt. "Maybe so. But a little ladybug casts a long shadow."

The Dictator lifted a hand to swat Lew, but the baroness had been squinting at the detective through her monocle. "Wait, Raoul. A detective, is he? I have need of a sharp-eyed spy. What do you say, bug? Will you serve me?"

Lew kept quiet as if thinking. Finally—to my surprise and horror—he asked, "What's in it for me, lady?"

"How much are you making?" demanded the baroness.

"Thirty-five aphids a day, plus expenses."

"Very well, I'll pay you forty. Turn down my offer and"—she made a pinch in the air with thumb and forefinger—"you perish. Take it or leave it. Well?"

"I'll take it. When do I start?"

"Lew!" my sister wailed in agony. "Lew, you can't walk out on us! You can't quit us and go work for this—this witch—just for five more aphids! Why, whatever will Gran think of you?"

The baroness flashed her rat-teeth. "Every bug has his price. All right, detective, you're hired. Come sit on my shoulder."

And without another word, Lew sailed over to her. Oh, it was a bad hour. To see our small friend on the side of the enemy made me sick at heart. I couldn't believe he had abandoned us. As ever, his insect face wore no expression at all, but for a moment I could have sworn that, from his roost on Ratisha's shoulder, he had thrown me a wink. And yet—how could he? His eyes didn't have any lids.

The Dictator settled back in his chair, lit a gray cigarette, and spat out a vile-smelling cloud. "Remove these brats. Take 'em and throw 'em in the mine and let 'em shovel muck till their backs snap."

"Only the boy goes to the mine," the baroness corrected. "I'm keeping the girl. I know a use for her."

"All right," Raoul agreed carelessly, "and throw

the bear into the meat locker. He'll do for steak when he has been properly marinated. His skin can make Ratisha a stuffed animal to take to bed at night. Now bring me a pot of coffee with some beer in it."

10. *In the Mountain's Cellar*

The elevator wasn't much more than an owlstone box. It fell down—down—down—till at last it jerked to a stop.

"Out!" said the tall owl, so out I stepped, and sank up to my ankles in cold water.

The mine was no easier to see around in than Raoul's dining room. As I stood there trying to focus, a shape rolled up out of the dark. It was another tall owl, the one in charge. It carried a shovel in its beak, the way a dog will carry a stick, and when it got within six feet of me it flung the shovel at my head. By luck, I made the catch.

"Prisoner eighty-seven-two-o-eight," my escort announced me. "His Vileness wishes this prisoner to work here until his back snaps."

The other flashed its eye-cells, recording my number. "Prisoner," it droned to me, "you will notify me as soon as your back has snapped."

Then the boss owl raised a wing and swatted

me into my place in a long row of bent-over slaves. By the flickering light, I could tell they were digging with shovels and slinging wet muck onto carts. There were people of every kind—women and girls, men and boys, and they came in all ages. They were ragged and skinny and plastered with muck, like a lot of shaggy, dripping, slowly moving animals. Because the mine was chilling cold, they were coughing and wheezing and snuffling. Their job was to keep filling carts. Tall owls stood guard over them, and any worker who took a moment off to rest soon felt the jab of a beak. The carts, when filled, slid along a rail and hooked onto a moving chain and climbed up out of sight, lifting the muck, no doubt, to the factory that made more stone owls. Like overgrown bats, muckhawks kept thrashing by, just missing our heads, shrieking and pooping and adding to the general misery. All you could hear were cold-symptoms and muckhawk wings, the drip of water, the groan of loaded carts.

The only light came from buckets of oil suspended from iron spikes, that burned with unsteady blue flames. It was enough to show the tunnel's ceiling and walls, all twined with pale white tubes like macaroni, only thicker than sewer-pipes. These, I found out later, were the roots of the gigantic Moonflower.

So there I stood, cold muck-juice soaking my shoes, never again to see Verity or Gran or

Gramp! I was starting to feel a hopeless, squeezed-in feeling. And to think that Lew, faithful Lew, had sold out on us! Almost as bad was the thought of Fardels, his bushy skin stuffed with cotton, his kindly eyes traded for buttons, as a teddybear in the Baroness Ratisha's bed! Maybe I've had worse moments in my life than that one, but I don't remember any.

Once, I read this book by a Frenchman about these two twin brothers who could feel what each other felt. When one was being tortured, the other, a hundred miles away, woke up hollering. I shut my eyes and tried to tell if Verity, wherever she was, felt anything special. But all I could feel was the ice water trickling down my backbone, dripping from the ceiling of the mine.

Maybe I'd keep warm if I worked faster. I drove my shovel into the muck at my feet and hoisted a glob of the stuff, which came loose with a *SUCK-KK-K-K!* Savagely, I slung it into the nearest cart.

"What's your hurry?" asked a voice at my right elbow. "Slow down, or you'll wear yourself out."

The friendly voice had come from the shoveler next to me. He turned his face my way, and I took it in by the light of the oil-bucket overhead. He was just a kid, younger than me, with tumbledown hair and a grin that shone through his falseface of mud.

"Can you be Wildmustard Weedblossom?" I asked him.

"You're right. Mustard, to my friends. How come you know me?"

"You look like your mother. The same mustard-colored hair. And you both have one green eye and the other brown."

I told him how we'd met his mother on the highway, and he pressed me for news of her, and I gave him what little I could.

"Timothy Tibb!" he kept repeating. "That's a funny name. Hey, look, Timothy Tibb, here come our ten o'clock muckolates!"

An owl with a big stone jar was rolling along our line, pausing at every shoveler. Each person held out a hand for some little dark objects to rattle into. When the owl came to Mustard and me, we stuck out our hands, and the jar poured and the owl rolled on, and Mustard cried, "Chug-a-lug!" and gulped his ration.

"What are they?" I asked suspiciously, sniffing my handful of clay-colored jellybeans.

"Muck pills. They're really rotten, but they're all the breakfast, lunch, and dinner you're going to get."

I tried one. It tasted like a mudpie that, on a dare, I had once eaten in kindergarten. But I was starving. I opened wide and tossed down all the rest.

Right away my stomach began to play leapfrog. Soon I was throwing up.

"You'll be all right, Timothy Tibb," said Mustard gently. "Everybody gets sick the first time. You'll get used to them."

I decided I'd much rather starve.

From behind my back, now, came a sudden rumble. I spun, to see a frightening machine go wallowing by. It was owlstone-gray, the size of an army tank, and it moved on a rotating tread. On the end of its nose, a drill was whirling.

"That's an owlstone mole," Mustard told me. "Some new kind of weapon, I guess."

The mole slogged on through the muck till it came to a wall. But it didn't stop. It just drilled its way through that solid rock like a corkscrew put to a cheese. Then it rumbled on into the hole it had bored, and the darkness swallowed it.

Despite my new friend's reputation for making trouble—trouble for the tomato-farmer's cows, at least—I soon decided that Mustard Weed-blossom was all right. If you had heard him kidding with the other slaves, cheering them up, you'd have thought so too. In our work gang there were some frail-looking old gentlemen. Once, when one of them keeled right over, worn out from shoveling, Mustard barged over to him and helped him to his feet again, and for a long while the kid not only did his own shoveling, he did the old gent's shoveling besides.

Mustard's good-humored gab improved that dismal mine. As we worked side by side, not very fast, I told him my story, and he told me his.

After the owls had arrested his father, Mustard had made a beeline for the Hall to try to rescue him, but had been promptly captured. I told him about me and Verity and Lew, and when the younger kid heard how Fardels had trashed six owls in front of the Dictator, he threw a laughing fit. Then and there, he and I made a vow to be brothers, and we shook on it, locking our little fingers. While we were sealing this pact, a suspicious owl rolled over and lightly pecked at us. We went back to our shovels again and worked hard until the owl, satisfied, rolled away.

"That old owl," said Mustard, "hardly can peck any more. Its gears must be wearing smooth. Guess it was the first owl Dad ever built."

"Huh? Your dad built it? I thought Raoul invented stone owls."

"Raoul couldn't invent a thumbtack. My dad was the one that discovered owlstone in the first place. He cooked up a batch of the stuff, and at first he didn't know what shape to put it into. Then one day Raoul came along, a stranger. He looked so much like an owl that Dad had him pose, and Dad modeled the stone owls after him."

"That figures. I thought Raoul and the owls looked a lot alike. But what did your dad want to invent those mean things for?"

"Dad meant the owls to help people. To catch mice in farmers' barns—gently, not hurting the mice, of course. But then Raoul changed everything. He stole the secret recipe for making owls, and he took Dad prisoner. If only I knew where Dad was!"

Three bent backs down the line from me, a middle-aged man let out a strangling gasp, pitched forward on his shovel, and lay still. Mustard made a jump over to help him, but the old owl, with a swat of one wing, knocked the kid aside. Two more owls picked up the collapsed miner by the feet and dragged him away into the dark. When they came back, they had a fresh miner in between them, to replace the one who'd worn out.

"Keep away, you statues," said the replacement. "I don't need to be forced."

And he took up the shovel of the fallen miner, and he gave it an expert thrust into the muck. When he bobbed up again, he stood straight as a flagpole. His hair was so white it sparkled, even under the feeble light.

I'd seen this man before.

My heart tried to leap into my throat.

"GRAMP!" I yelled. "Is it really *you?*"

Oh, it really was my grandfather, all right. Nobody had whiter hair or stood straighter or talked that way, making every word count. At my shout, Gramp whirled, and he saw me. He let out a beautiful grin.

"TIM!" he bellowed, loud enough to bring every owl in the mine.

I flung down my shovel and started toward

him. I wanted to throw myself at him and hug him half to death.

"I'm coming, Gramp!" I hollered.

But I wasn't going. A weight—it must have been an owlstone wing—slammed into the back of my head. I dropped to the floor of the muck mine like ten tons.

11. *A Poison Seethes*

NOTE BY TIM: *While I was having my troubles down in the mine, big things were happening up in the kitchen of Owlstone Hall. But I'll let Verity tell you about them. She was there.*

You understand, I'm not an experienced storyteller, like Timmy. I'm going to tell you the truth. After the owl went rolling away with my brother—I knew they were gone, because the floor shook and then it stopped shaking—the Baroness Ratisha von Bad Radisch said to me, "This way, girl! We'll see how much work you have in you! Step along, step along!"

She pinched hold of my ear and dragged me with her. Behind us, a door bumped shut. Then we were in the kitchen—as I guessed from all the sour old cooking smells. The baroness shoved me in the back of the neck and I stumbled forward into something that clicked against my belt buckle. It was a sink.

She said, "Now, my tender chicken, you shall stand there and scrub those pots until they shine like diamonds. DIAMONDS, I say!"

Tender chicken, huh? I could have strangled her. And how could I know when her dumb pots shone? With my glasses missing, I could hardly tell day from night.

I said, "You can't mean it. You aren't really going to throw Timmy in the muck mine till his back snaps, are you? You aren't going to soak Fardels Bear in vinegar and make steaks out of him."

"Oh, aren't we?" said the baroness, with a laugh I didn't like. "Muck is the very thing for boys, the noisy monsters. As for that filthy bear with his muzzle all sticky—ugh! Marination is too good for him. But Raoul has his heart set on a bear steak dinner. Now get busy—scrub!"

What could I do? I asked her for a scouring pad, but there wasn't any. She said, "Haven't you any fingernails? Use them to dig!"

That struck me as a mean thing to ask of anybody, so I said I wouldn't do it. The baroness didn't like that. She ordered me to look into her monocle. I guess she wanted to hypnotize me, the way she had done to Fardels, but I told her it wouldn't work. I was practically blind, didn't she know? I couldn't even see her old monocle. That made her just furious. She threw me a slap on the cheek that stung. I warned her, "Look out, don't make me mad, or you'll be sorry."

Oh, what a nasty, shrieking laugh she gave. "*I* should fear *you*? A puny little string bean who is blind?"

That did it. I'm not puny. After all, I was wrestling champ of our junior high. I shot out my arms to where her voice was coming from, took her around the neck, threw a half-nelson on her, flipped her up in the air, and slammed her down. It was easy. She didn't weigh very much at all.

For a long time the baroness lay there with her breath knocked out. At last I heard her scramble to her feet.

"For that, my fine chicken, the muckhawks shall tear you to tatters. No, no, that won't do—I want you to die by slow degrees. *You will scrub pots.*"

"You can't make me."

"Oh, can't I? Do you know, I'm holding your friend the ladybug between my thumb and my pointing finger. Shall I crush him, or will you do as I say?"

I thought about it. Lew was a traitor. He had let the baroness buy him away from us. I was ready to say, "Go ahead, crush him," when I remembered how good he had always used to be.

"All right." I gave in. "I'll scrub pots."

"That's better. Dip those pretty fingers into that kettle and scrape. Now as for you, ladybug—"

"At your service, ma'am," Lew said politely. "You wanted some detecting?"

The baroness lowered her voice. "Listen, bug. I have reason to believe that old Aspen Appleyard, the eldest Elder, suspects me of plotting against his life. Of course, his fears are ridiculous. But I don't trust him. I think he is planning trouble for us. You will fly to his home—do you know it?"

"Yeah. He lives in a treehouse in the big orchard south of here."

"Exactly. I want you to hide there and eavesdrop on everything he says. You will report back to me."

"Right, Your Highness." A tiny flurry in the air told me that the detective had taken off. Oh, the turncoat! I could have pinched him to a pulp.

"Aha, very good, the poison is now bubbling," Ratisha was telling her chef. "You will stir it slowly with your wing for the next seven hours. Put in a few dried serpent tongues from this jar. Serpent tongues add zest."

"Execrable, Madam," said the owl.

While the poison-chef was getting its briefing, I kept trying to scrape the crust of some old soup from the bottom of an iron kettle. I could hear splashes inside the kettle. They must have been my tears.

Now, you understand, I didn't feel sorry for myself. That wasn't it. I was just so boiling mad— to be so helpless, at such a time! Then, all of a sudden, from out of my back pocket, a shrill little voice said, "Don't. Cry. Verity. —Couldn't. Things. Be. Worse?"

"Huh! A lot you know about it, Shelley Snail! Worse? How could things be? Timmy and Fardels are someplace being put to death. Lew is working for the baroness. She's boiling some terrible-smelling stuff to poison somebody. We're never going to rescue Gran and Gramp. My glasses are lost and I can't see a thing, and I'm never going to get the crust out of this scuzzy old soup kettle."

"I'm. Sorry."

"Oh, Shelley, forgive me, what a no-good friend I am. I'd forgotten you. Aren't you hungry?"

"Yes. Please. I. Am. Famished. —Please. Set. Me. Down. On. That. Cart. Full. Of. Mildewed. Cabbages."

My nose soon led me to the cart it meant. I felt around, found the biggest and soggiest cabbage, and without the baroness noticing, set Shelley down on it.

Just then, heavy footfalls came into the kitchen. A panting and wheezing, and the flapping of wings. The Dictator had arrived, no doubt with his pet muckhawk, as usual.

"Gaze!" he cried out in a deep, commanding voice. "Gaze upon me, Ratisha! Did you ever see such a magnificent thing in your life?"

The baroness gave a surprised gasp. "Why, Raoul, the crown—it looks perfectly dreadful! I mean that," she quickly added, "as a compliment.

And the snakeskin—yes, it glitters beautifully. But where are the jewels?"

"Oh, the crown isn't finished. It still needs its sparklers set into place. Weedblossom is working on it. But I just had to borrow it from the laboratory for a minute and give you a preview of me. Me—in my owlstone crown! The Emperor of Owlstonia!"

I couldn't see the crown Raoul was wearing, of course, but owlstone, snakeskin, and jewels—that sounded horrible.

After he had paraded around in front of the baroness for a while, Raoul told an owl to take the crown back to the laboratory. Weedblossom should get moving on it. Then the clanging and banging of pot lids told me that the Dictator was looking into kettles, to find out what was for lunch.

One kettle made him just about retch. He said, "Ratty, this stuff had better not be for ME to eat. Are you trying to poison somebody?"

"Yes, of course. We must prepare the refreshments for your coronation, must we not? We are brewing a tasteless little substance that will work with lightning speed. Soon you'll have no enemies."

"Good. I knew I could depend on you. Just don't put the wrong kind of flowers on the refreshment table. What if—ULP!"

His words stopped in a gurgle, as though the baroness had clamped a hand across his mouth.

"You idiot, Raoul," she said to him. "You nearly gave away the secret of Owlstone Hall in front of this big-eared little pot-scrubber!"

At that, I *was* all ears. What secret could she mean? And what did flowers have to do with it?

Well, they rattled on about this and that, and Raoul said, "Do you realize, Ratty, that our dream is about to come true? A land all to ourselves! A land of owls, with just me and you—the only two people alive!"

"Shelley, do you hear that?" I said to the snail on its cabbage. "How can we stop them in time?"

The baroness had heard me. "You, girl, what are you doing at the cabbage cart? Who is that you're talking to?"

"My snail Shelley," I said. "The poet and the prophet."

You see, I never deny anything that will only be found out.

At my words, Raoul sounded all interested. He must have picked up Shelley in his hand. "Snail," he said in a soft wheedling voice, "are you the kind that knows what is to come?"

"I. Can. Foresee. Most. Things," Shelley said.

"Aha! This is my lucky day! I've always wanted to meet a snail like you. All right, snail—Raoul Owlstone commands you. Look into my future. What do you see?"

"You. Are. A. Large. Order," said Shelley. "Your. Future. Will. Take. Me. A. While."

"Then start!"

A long silence fell in the kitchen, except for the Dictator, grumbling impatiently. After many minutes, Shelley's high voice piped:

Stone. Owls. Shall. Roll. Till. Owlstone. Walls. Dissolve.

And. Raoul. Rule. Till. Moonflower. Mount. Revolve!

"Hmmm," said Raoul, trying to think. "*Till Moonflower Mount Revolve,* eh? Who ever heard of such a thing? Mountains don't revolve. They're not on turntables. Bah! that couldn't happen in a million years. Ratty, do you understand? This wise snail says I'm going to rule forever!"

A clapping, whooping and stomping told me the Dictator was doing a dance all around the floor. *Awwkk-k-k!* cried his muckhawk in alarm.

"Fool," said the baroness. "Surely you don't believe a fortune-telling snail!"

"Why not? Everybody knows snails never lie. Come on, snail—tell us Ratty's fortune too!"

This time, Shelley's prediction was worth waiting for:

Before. Day's. End. A. Stranger. Shall. Let. Fly.

A. Punch To. Close. Ratisha's. Spinning. Eye.

"Why, you little slime," said the baroness.

The prediction didn't make a bit of sense to me. Raoul gave a hooting laugh. "Too bad for you, Ratty! Anyway, MY fortune is beautiful! Raoul shall rule till Moonflower Mount revolves! Long live Emperor Raoul! Long live me!"

And trying to skip with joy—and stumbling—he left the room.

No sooner was he gone than the baroness said to Shelley, in a cold, threatening voice, "So, snail. You foresee a splendid future for Raoul and an insulting one for me. I'll fix YOUR future for you!"

What was she going to do? I had to save Shelley! I flung myself in the direction of her voice. Squinting as hard as I could, I could make out a dim blur. The blur was reaching high, swinging—

I made a grab for it.

Too late.

A gust of wind blew into the room from an open window-slot.

Tears stung my cheeks. I wailed, "What did you do? Where's Shelley?"

The baroness gave a laugh that ran up and down all the scales. "So, little chicken, you're worried about your snail, are you? Well, you won't have to worry any more. I have thrown it out of the window. By now it's smashed to powder. From here to the rocks at the foot of the mountain, there's a drop of a quarter of a mile."

12. *I Fulfill a Prophecy*

It's me, Tim, again. After the owl slammed me over the head I must have taken a nap. When I woke up I was lying on my back on the mine floor listening to a faint, familiar twittering. A tiny breeze was blowing down on me, as if from a pea-sized electric fan. Slowly, everything focused. The twitter was Lew, hovering over me and fanning me with his wings.

"Kid, are you OK?" he rasped.

The back of my head felt like a mine cave-in. "I—I'll live," I answered. "Lew, what are YOU doing here? I thought you took a better-paying job with the baroness."

"Wrong," grunted the detective. "I didn't work for that witch. I only pretended to, till I could slip away. Your sister's OK. She's up in the kitchen scrubbing pots."

Then the whole past rushed back to me. I sat

up. "Gramp!" I cried. "Where's Gramp? I saw him, Lew, I really did!" My head hurt.

"Not so fast, kid," Lew said gently. "Yeah, yeah, you saw your grandfather, all right. Only he isn't around anymore—the owls moved him to a different tunnel. Guess they figured he was disturbing the peace."

With the help of an arm from Mustard, I struggled to my feet. Weak though I was, I was hopping mad and I wanted to fight. "They took Gramp away! I'll fix them!" But my head felt as though it had a steam drill pounding on it.

Lew barked from my collar, "Calm down, kid. In a minute the owls will notice you're awake, and they'll throw you and Mustard back on the shovels. But before they do, we're getting out of here. I know, see, where the exit is."

"Lew, I can't go. I've got to find Gramp again. Where did they take him to?"

"Listen, junior, get your head on straight. This is no time to play raiding party. You stick around here much longer and you'll dig muck till you rot. Which won't do your grandfather any good, especially."

"That's right, Timothy Tibb," Mustard said urgently, "you've got to come along."

Two wishes were battling inside of me. What should I do? Try to save Gramp all by myself? Or escape, then try to rescue Gramp and the other miners? It was too big a problem at the moment. Dizzy as a washed cat, I sat back down in the muck.

"On your feet, Tibb!" snarled the detective. "Don't pass out, for crying out loud! You've got to walk another thirty or forty yards."

My eyes blurred—cleared—blurred again.

"I won't go," I said as firmly as possible. "Can't run out on Gramp. Only just saw my Gramp again."

"We'll come back!" Mustard promised. "Right now you've got to come with Lew and me. Remember, Timothy Tibb, we have to stick together, you and me! We're brothers—don't you remember? You swore!"

Half-dragging, half-carrying me, he was moving me along the corridor, while I kept trying to pass out and slide back down in the muck. But at last we were standing before a wooden door in the tunnel wall—a door maybe two feet square. Mustard yanked it open. I stared into a square hole full of darkness.

"I won't go," I said.

Lew blew up at me. "Listen, Tibb, you stick your foot through that door before I haul off and beat the American Beauty roses out of you. Move!"

Once more, the mine was slipping out of focus. As I stood there swaying, a tall owl caught sight of us. Now it came speeding toward us, eye-cells flashing. "*You! Prisoners! Halt!*"

Somehow, that decided me. I lifted a leg into

the dark open doorway, and Mustard gave me a boost and he shoved me right on through. Lew darted in, and Mustard climbed in behind me, and only seconds before the owl reached us, the kid slammed the little wooden door.

We had squeezed ourselves into a pitch-dark compartment, so narrow that my elbows bumped its sides. I groped down and felt a platform under my feet.

I said, "Lew, where are we?"

"In a dumbwaiter, kid—Raoul's personal food elevator. Just make believe you're a tray of chicken sandwiches."

"Then you mean we can ride up on it?"

"You catch on quick, sweetheart. How's your head?"

It was better. In fact, it suddenly cleared altogether, with a *poof!* like a cap coming off a soda bottle. But still, we were in trouble. In the cavern outside, the owl was bawling, "Prisoners have escaped!"—while it kept up a steady thunder on the dumbwaiter door. That door would have crashed in on us, no doubt, if Mustard and I hadn't thrown our shoulders against it. Splinters were raining in on us, and soon a crack of light appeared in the door right where the owl's beak must have been bopping it.

Mustard sounded worried. "The owl is busting through!"

"Yank the rope," Lew urged from my collar.

Two ropes, in fact, hung in front of me. I could feel them in the dark, so I grabbed the closer one and yanked down on it. High over our heads, an invisible wheel creaked, and underneath us the platform lurched, and we climbed a few inches up a narrow shaft.

"That's the way, Timothy!" Mustard breathed, "you pull down, I'll pull up."

You had better believe we fell to tugging on those ropes like a couple of busy demons. Lew rasped encouragement—"Heave, heave, you mutts!" and "Will you PULL, you lazy palookas?"

Soon the dumbwaiter, which hung from a pulley, was climbing steadily. From under us came a huge CRASH as the door caved in, and then the owl was hooting up the shaft at us:

"Stop! Do not escape! It is not ordered!"

I was pulling as hard as I knew how, and yet for some reason, we had stopped climbing.

"We're stuck," I quavered. My old fears of dark closed-in places were swooping back to me.

"Rats," said Lew with feeling. "What do you bet that that owl has caught hold of the ropes?"

"Let me try something," said Mustard. It was so dark I didn't know what he tried, but in a few seconds there came a loud CRUNCH from the shaft directly below.

"Pull some more now, Timothy," Mustard told me, and I pulled and he pulled, and sure enough, up we went.

"What did you do to that owl?" I wanted to know.

The kid guffawed. "Dropped my shovel on it."

As we kept on tugging and hauling and the platform kept on rising with us, I wondered out loud what a dumbwaiter was doing down in a mine. "Raoul," explained Mustard, "likes to visit the mine and watch the slavery. Naturally, he has food sent down to him. One time I saw him strutting around our tunnel munching a whole ham like it was an apple."

We had risen into a beam of dim gray light. It fell from a horizontal slot at the top of the shaft overhead. My hands were sore from the rope, but I kept on pulling until at last, puffing and gasping, we had worked our platform up to the level of the slot. When we got there, we saw that a downward-sliding door had been left open a crack, giving us a slot just wide enough to peer out through.

To my big surprise, I found myself looking out into the kitchen of Owlstone Hall. At a deep sink, Verity was scrubbing a frying pan with her fingernails. Smack in front of me stood Raoul Owlstone and the skully-looking baroness and four stone owls.

"It's Verity!" I whispered. "We've got to save her!"

But how? We had no weapons. I searched my

pockets, but all I could find was an old unstuck label for parsnip punch.

"Will you look at that," said the detective. "Something funny's happening."

Raoul and Ratisha and the owls were standing around a table that had a muckhawk lying on it. "Chuckles, baby," the Dictator cooed, "Chuckles, chick. Does Daddy's lovely muckhawk have a tummyache?"

Well, it gave ME a tummyache to hear such a fuss made over that dirty bird. Chuckles Baby weakly lifted his head, croaked horribly, and bleated, "Gut hurt! Chuckles gut hurt!" then he fell back flat again.

"Scruffy thing looks ready for the dump," said the baroness with a sniff.

"No, no!" Raoul said quickly. "This must be just something he ate. Owls, turn him upside down and shake him out."

Two owls grabbed the muckhawk by the feet and hung him up in the air, head dangling. Mechanically, they swung him to and fro while Raoul kept slapping his back like a doctor trying to get a newborn baby to start working. After a little of this treatment, the muckhawk let out a burp. A round yellowish thing dropped from his open beak and rattled down onto the table.

Shelley!

The snail poked its head out of its shell and

made a face. "Ugggghh! I've. A. Terrible. Taste. In. My. Mouth—Would. Someone. Put. Me. Back. On. That. Mildewed. Cabbage?"

Verity was jumping for joy.

"Cabbage, indeed!" shrieked the baroness. "You slimy leaf-licker, I thought I had got rid of you!"

At that, Raoul pricked up his pointed ears. "What's that? Tell me, snail, what did the baroness do to you?"

"She. Threw. Me. Out. Of. The. Window-slot. But. Chuckles. Caught. Me. In. Midair. Thinking. I. Was. Some. Tasty. Morsel."

"Liar!" said the baroness, twitching nervously.

"So, Ratty," said the Dictator, glowering, "you tried to do away with this snail. This prophet who sees a fine future for me. My poor Chuckles almost died of indigestion. This time, Ratty, you've gone too far."

The baroness turned whiter than usual. "Now, Raoul, remember, I'm your Empress-to-be—"

The Dictator took a menacing step toward her, but the baroness blazed her rose-red monocle. The eyepiece spun, and Raoul stared into it. In a moment he quieted down.

"I—I forget," he said, "what I was angry about."

"That's all right, my dear," the baroness said oilily. "You were excited about saving Chuckles, that's all. Why don't you go take a nap?"

"Good idea," said the Dictator vacantly. Picking up his pet, he placed the muckhawk back on his shoulder and left the kitchen without another word. I had to hand it to that monocle. It made even Raoul behave like a good dog.

Verity had groped around on the table and found Shelley. Tenderly, she wiped the snail's shell dry with her handkerchief and returned the little mollusk to her pocket.

"Owls!" shrieked the baroness. "Grab that girl and her snail! Throw them BOTH out the window!"

Naturally, none of us inside the dumbwaiter wanted *that* to happen. "*Let's go!*" I yelled.

Mustard flung up the sliding door, and he and I exploded into the kitchen. We hit the floor in front of the baroness. She took one look at us and screamed. No doubt we were an awful sight, being slathered with mine-muck from head to toe.

The owls just stood there blinking their eye-cells, awaiting orders. The baroness reacted in a flash.

"Gaze!" she commanded, glaring hard at me and Mustard. "Gaze into my monocle!"

In her right eye socket, the rose-red glass began to spin. Despite myself, I couldn't tear my eyes from it. Lew was beating the air in front of my face, crying, "Tim! Tim! Shut your eyes!"

I shut my eyes and reopened them. That snapped me to my senses. But Mustard looked asleep on his feet.

"Do as I say," the red-and-white witch crooned to him.

What could I do? My fingers tightened around the only weapon I had—the GRIMBLE'S PARSNIP PUNCH label still in my pocket. I'd try anything! I whipped it out and gave it a speedy lick. I stepped right up to the baroness. With a thrust, I pasted the sticky label on top of her spinning monocle.

Mustard woke, as if he'd been sloshed with a bucketful of icewater.

NOTE BY VERITY: *Remember what Shelley predicted? A stranger—that was Timmy—had let fly a punch to close Ratisha's eye, all right, all right.*

The baroness let out a gurgle. "You fool, you've broken the spell! You—you—you—you *CHILD!*"

Out of her good eye, then, she spied Lew on my collar. "Two-timing gumshoe," she flung at him. "Have you betrayed me?"

"Don't break my heart, sister," grunted Lew. "Remind me to laugh at you on my day off."

Three stone owls rumbled toward us. I didn't like the gleam in their electric eyes.

"Follow me, kids!" the detective barked.

"Sis, grab my shirt-tail!" I cried.

We ran for our lives. We kicked open the nearest door and went barging out into a shadowy, unknown corridor.

13. *Ominous Inventions*

BRR-RR-RRANNG-G-G!

Somewhere in the corridor an alarm bell jangled. A loudspeaker started to hoot in Raoul's hollow voice:

Intruders! Intruders in the Hall! All owls report to the kitchen! NOW!"

Mustard, my sister, and I were legging down that corridor like crazy, while my heart kept trying to break out through my chest. Lew, scouting the corridor ahead of us, made a U-turn in the air and cried, "Owls coming! Run the other way!"

A rumble was heading toward us. We whirled around, but now a second rumble was coming from the corridor behind us, too. The owls had us in a squeeze. They were closing in on us from both directions.

All I could see was a sign on a door:

LABORATORY
KEEP OUT

Well, I wouldn't keep out. I grabbed a handle and tugged, and the heavy door swung outward. Then we were inside the laboratory, a high-ceilinged room all glitter and glass, hearing the door thud shut after us, hearing our pulses beat like drums, hearing—outside in the corridor—two thunders of owls roll by.

A man in a long white coat strode toward us—a lean, pale, youngish man with a chin that hadn't been shaved lately. From behind horn-rimmed glasses he blinked at us intently, as if we were specimens fallen from Mars.

"Who are you?" he demanded briskly.

"We—we're the intruders," said Verity, panting. "The owls—they're after us. Can you let us hide?"

The all-in-white man—I guessed he was some kind of scientist—removed a forgotten pipe from

his jaw. I expected him to holler for the guards.
Just as I was screwing up my courage to jump
him and try to beat him up, his face broke into
a beautiful big wide grin. He was looking straight
past Verity and me. At Mustard.

Then, didn't he and Mustard fling themselves
at each other and pound each other's backs.

"Dad! Dad!" Mustard was yelling.

"Son, where've you been lately?"

Well, you're right. The man in the white coat
was Mustard's father, Oak Weedblossom, the inventor of owlstone and stone owls. He couldn't
believe it was really his son standing there, and
it wasn't any wonder he couldn't, because Mustard was covered with mine-muck from head to
foot. Now the pair of them were jabbering, laughing, trading news. They were so wrapped up in
each other I began to feel out of place. Mustard
had a dad and I didn't. Down in the mine, I had
found my grandfather. But for only a minute, no
more.

Then Mustard introduced us all around, not
leaving out Shelley, and he told his father how
he and I had sworn to be brothers. Dr. Weedblossom pumped my hand in the warmest way,
and he let me know I was welcome in his laboratory, and Lew and the snail and Verity besides.

"In fact," he said cheerfully, "you picked the
right place to hide. The owls won't look for you

here. They're under orders from Raoul not to bother me. You see, I'm supposed to be thinking."

"About what?" Verity wanted to know.

"About inventions. I'm supposed to think up a new one every day." He groaned. "As if I hadn't invented enough terrible things already."

"Like stone owls?" my sister asked brightly.

"Don't rub it in." The inventer sighed, and looked sorrowful.

Even though stone owls were the pits, in my opinion, I wanted to ask for his autograph. I hadn't ever met a real live inventor before. Only because Mustard begged, Dr. Weedblossom showed us around his laboratory. Not that he acted the least bit proud of what he was working on. There was a noise machine that, at the flick of a switch, gave out a clatter like slammed-down trash cans. Raoul planned to use it to drown out some waterfall. There was a machine for making smoke out of morning mist and another for giving roses a rotten egg smell. But the strangest and most terrible object of all sat on a workbench. Just to look at it gave me the shakes.

"That," said Dr. Weedblossom when I asked him, "is the owlstone crown. The baroness designed the awful thing. When I've finished, Raoul will crown himself Emperor. That will be a grim day, for then he'll destroy the last of his enemies."

"And who are they?"

"Oh, the Elders, of course. Months ago, the baroness hypnotized them into naming Raoul the Dictator, but lately they've been growing rebellious. No doubt Ratisha is cooking up a way to put them to death."

"She certainly is," Verity put in. "She's cooking poison. I got a whiff of it."

A fresh chill went racing to my shoes. I stared at the owlstone crown. Round and gray and icy-looking, it squatted on the workbench like some giant horned toad that had slithered out of a freezer. From all around its rim, sharp spikes, each a foot tall and pointed like an icicle, stabbed the air. A dome of glittery silver snakeskin bulged up from inside its headband to cover the wearer's scalp. On the forehead, two jewels were fixed, green-and-yellow stones like the eyes of a snarling cat. More of the same lay loose on the workbench, waiting to join the rest. All in all, the crown glowed with cold, evil power. I shivered again and turned my back on it.

But we had another bad scene in store for us. Dr. Weedblossom fingered a button and the whole rear wall of his laboratory slid aside, and there it was, taking up the back half of Owlstone Hall— the stone owl factory. Assuring us that the workers wouldn't pay us any notice, Mustard's father led us out onto a balcony to watch the action below. No people worked in that factory, just hundreds of tireless owls. Around and around the owlstone floor they rolled with a steady boom, like a rink full of roller skaters. Carts of muck kept arriving from the mine on an endless chain, and the owls kept dumping them into the hoppers of machines to turn out pills and grenades and bombs. Half-finished owls, riding along on a moving belt, were being sandblasted smooth and having bills stuck to their heads and ball-bearings fixed to their bottoms. Stone eggs were being assembled, too, and stone moles with drills, like the one I had seen chew through a wall in the mine.

In the middle of the tremendous room stood a furnace as tall as Owlstone Hall itself. Worker owls were dumping fuel into it. This fuel, I was told, consisted of toys, books, magazines, paintings, boxes of candy, letters that hadn't been delivered—anything that would have made somebody glad. The furnace cooked all the owlstone used in the country. And what was owlstone made of? Fog, ice, muck, and polluted water. The furnace gurgled. You couldn't see its fires.

At last, our eyes smarting from the dust and our ears beaten down with the din, we returned to the quiet laboratory, and the rear wall slid back into place. Dr. Weedblossom looked glum. "To think I had to invent owlstone," he moaned. "To think I had to build stone owls. All I ever meant to do was make a better mousetrap. Now look at all the misery I've caused."

"It isn't your fault, Dad," said Mustard loyally. "Owls were a good invention. Raoul just used it wrong."

Verity flared up. "Excuse me, but I think it is your fault, Dr. Weedblossom! At least *some* of it. Why do you keep working for Raoul Owlstone? Why do you have to invent *more* of these terrible things? You could stop inventing terrible things, you know."

Looking cornered, Dr. Weedblossom tugged his chin stubble and chewed on his empty pipe. His answer came slowly, as if he didn't much want to let go of it. "All right. I guess I *am* to blame. You see, Raoul told me that unless I kept inventing things, harm would come to Wildmustard and to my wife. Don't you understand? I wanted to protect my loved ones. And so I did what Raoul and Ratisha told me to. I built stone eggs for the owls to ride in. I made muck-bombs for them to throw."

"Yes, and they threw one at *our* house," said Mustard sadly. "Dad, you shouldn't have helped Raoul. You shouldn't have worried just about Mom and me. You should have worried about the whole world."

"That's very hard for a human person to do, Mustard," said Verity.

Dr. Weedblossom looked so sorry that Mustard sat down next to him and put his arms around him. The inventor kept murmuring, "Why? Why didn't I see through Raoul's lies? If I had known he had bombed you and your mother, boy; if I had known he had sent you to the mine—! Your poor mother—oh, Heaven only knows what's become of her!"

"I know," put in Verity. "We met her on the highway yesterday. She's on her way here—to Owlstone Hall."

At this news, the scientist brightened. He stuck his pipe determinedly back into his jaw. "Then I'll find her. As for Raoul, I'm done with him! He'll never get another idea out of me!"

"Terrific, Dad," said Mustard. "By the way, is there anything to eat around here?"

Right away Dr. Weedblossom barked into a squawk-box and called for lunch. He ordered six times his usual amount of milk and sandwiches. "Oh, yes, and some aphids. I must have aphids! I'm starving!"

All of us intruders hid, and pretty soon in rolled the owl chef pushing a cart stacked high with sandwiches, peanut butter ones, and the tallest pitcher of chocolate milk you ever did see. For Lew, there was a red rose on a plate, its stem swarming with tiny white aphids. I could hear the detective on my collar smacking his lips.

NOTE BY VERITY: *Or whatever he could smack, Timmy ought to say.*

On its way out, the owl chef droned, "Doctor

Weedblossom, you will let no intruders into your laboratory. Raoul is searching for intruders. You will report at once if you should see any."

When the owl had gone, the inventor cried, "Dig in!" and the milk and sandwiches disappeared faster than a magician's rabbit. Lew, like a hungry dog gnawing a sparerib, skimmed up and down the stem of his rose till he had picked it clean.

After that good feed, and after Mustard and I had rinsed off our mine-muck in his father's showerbath, I felt greatly improved. But Verity looked crosser than ever.

"What now?" she demanded. "Here we are— stuck, trapped in this laboratory. And, oh, do you know what? Shelley made the worst prediction. Say it again, will you, Shelley?"

From her cupped hand the prophet intoned:

Stone. Owls. Shall. Roll. Till. Owlstone. Walls. Dissolve.

And. Raoul. Rule. Till. Moonflower. Mount. Revolve.

I stood stunned. What a scary forecast! Dr. Weedblossom puzzled his brows and said, "Hmmm, I don't see how a mountain can ever revolve. But owlstone, now—it can perish, you know."

"It can?" I yipped. "How do we make it perish?"

Just as the inventor of owlstone was opening

his mouth to answer, the loudspeaker over his workbench let out a squawk: "*Weedblossom!*" It was Raoul.

"Don't shout, I can hear you," said the inventor, frowning.

"Weedblossom, haven't you finished my crown yet?"

"Not yet."

"Back to work, Weedblossom! Get the thing done before I put you on a muck-pill diet. Wouldn't hurt you if I did, you gobbling swine. Oh, the chef owl told me what you ordered for lunch today. How can a grown man eat half a dozen peanut butter sandwiches? That's kid food. And how can you eat a roseful of aphids? That's bug food. By the way, Weedblossom, if you ever see three kids and a ladybug running around, let me know. They're escaped prisoners. One of the kids is named PARSNIP PUNCH. He pasted the Baroness von Bad Radisch with one of his calling cards. Tomorrow! I want my crown done by tomorrow! Tomorrow night's my coronation ball!"

14. *Prisoners at Large*

"If I know Raoul," Dr. Weedblossom said gloomily, "he'll be barging in here every five minutes to see that I finish his crown. This lab won't be a safe place for you to hide."

"Don't worry, Doc," Lew rasped. "We won't hang around here much longer. The heat's on, a whole army of owls is looking for us, and I know a place where these kids can lay low for a while. But first, I've got to get them out of this Hall."

"How? Every door is guarded."

"If we only had Fardels," Verity said wistfully. "He's the world's best owl-smasher."

Lew's compound eyes took on a crafty gleam. "Baby," he said to my sister, "you just hit on it. We're springing the bear."

"I know where Raoul keeps the zoo animals," said Dr. Weedblossom, eager to help. "They're all in cages in the meat locker, right next door."

"And how," I wondered, "do we unlock Fardels?"

"No problem," the inventor said. "Who do you think built every lock in Owlstone Hall? Me. Now, here"—he took down a key ring from a nail—"are the keys that open all the cages. Come on, let's release your friend right now."

"Hold on, Doc," the ladybug cut in gently. "We'd like to have you come with us, but you can't. You've got to stay here and work on Raoul's crown, or else he will miss you in a hurry. Take your sweet time finishing that bad hunk of ice, why don't you? I don't care, myself, if you never get it done."

"Then you're leaving?"

"Yeah. Soon as we jail-break the bear. I'm going to take these kids to a safer hiding place. A place where Raoul wouldn't look in a hundred years."

Now, Dr. Weedblossom was a brain, of course, and he saw that Lew was right. Just the same, he looked sad to have us go off without him. He hugged Mustard a whole lot and the rest of us to some extent, and he saluted Lew respectfully. He promised he'd try to stall Raoul and hold off finishing the owlstone crown for as long as possible. Our goodbyes said, the rest of us opened the laboratory door a crack and peered out into the corridor.

After a stone owl rumbled by, the coast was clear. We hurried to a door that said MEAT

LOCKER. In we went, into a racket of howls, chitters, growls, tweets, screams, gibbers and roars. In cages stacked to the ceiling, there were zebras and monkeys and wildebeests and—oh, about anything else you'd want to find in a zoo.

Off in a corner, hunched inside a cage four sizes too small, sat Fardels Bear. The minute we came in his kindly eyes glistened with joy.

"What took you guys so long to get here?" he said gruffly.

"We were waiting," Lew said dryly, "for you to be properly marinated."

I twisted key after key in the lock of his cage until one worked, and then the brown bear lumbered out happily. Verity flung her arms around his neck and tried squeezing the life out of him.

"Ooof!" grunted the bear. "Take it easy! Let me stretch, will you? My back has a kink in it."

Someone else had come slithering out of the cage, too—a bright green snake as thick as a fire hose. At the sight of it I wanted to turn and run, but the bear said, "Hey, meet my pal, Boswell. Boswell Boa Constrictor. That lying Raoul didn't grind him up for sausage after all."

"Pleas-ss-ss-ssed to meet you, I'm ss-ss-sure," the boa constrictor hissed.

My fear of the snake evaporated. I'd have been glad to shake hands with him, even, but that didn't seem possible.

"Say, you kids," called a gorilla from another

cage, "why don't you let us ALL out of here?"

"Why don't we?" I agreed. Lew thought it a good idea too. Maybe the zoo animals, running around loose, would keep the owls busy while we escaped from the Hall.

I turned every key on the key ring. Cages sprang open and the animals, loony with joy, came barging out. A mountain goat told me he'd never forget me. A chimpanzee gave me a kiss that tasted terrible. A river of fur and fangs overflowed the meat locker, bubbled on out the door, and soon filled the corridors of Owlstone Hall with bellows and roars and fearful trumpetings.

"OK, bear," Lew rasped, "we didn't spring you just because we like your looks. Think you can help us break out of this overgrown toadstool?"

The brown bear grinned. "Which way is the door?"

He and Mustard and Verity and I lit out down the nearest corridor, wading through a mob of happy animals. Four tall owls passed us, but didn't even pay us a glance. They were too busy trying to recapture a kangaroo.

All went well until we got to the Hall's big pair of front doors. A couple of sentinels stood guard. Extra-tall ones. They heard us coming. Their eye-cells flashing like angry traffic lights, they rumbled straight for us with their owlstone spears all ready to run us through.

Well, you know me. Naturally I started to trem-

ble. But the brown bear, with a wonderful growl, just reared up on his two hind feet and collected the pair of owls in his arms and bonked their heads together. Only one of the sentinels dropped. The other poked its spear into Fardels's belly. Luckily, the bear had thick skin. He just snarled, wrenched the spear away, and threw it clattering to the floor. Then he caught the owl in one shaggy arm and flung it down—KER-SMASH!—on top of its partner. It twitched and gave a faint hoot and lay still. A cloud of black dust rose from the owls' cracked batteries.

"You did it, Fardels!" yelped Mustard.

One swat of a heavy paw and the front doors flew wide open.

"Follow me, you mugs!" the detective cried. "I know a place a whole lot better than this!"

15. *Under the Dome*

"Drink," urged my grandmother, "drink, it's good for you. Slowly, now—not too fast. There isn't much to share with you today."

Gran was standing at the foot of the colossal Moonflower, pouring water out of an old paint bucket. She was soaking the soil right where the thick, twisting vines came out. She had on her painter's smock, leather boots, and the gold-and-green slacks she'd designed and dyed and woven all by herself. Now she was tucking a lock of salt-and-pepper hair up under her headband. As ever, her face was bright, with a ferocious, big-eyed look. The look I loved. A tan-colored bird, a mourning dove, perched on a vine, cooing and keeping her company.

She was facing my way, but she didn't see me. With Verity and Mustard and the brown bear, I was crouched down behind a boulder. We had

wriggled in under the thick glass dome, squeezing through a gap Lew knew about. We'd sneaked up on Gran, and we were going to give her the surprise of her life.

"It's so withered," Gran said aloud to herself. "Poor thing! I declare, it droops lower every day. Oh, if only I had more water! A couple of pitchers a day can't keep it alive..."

Sadly, she gazed up into the Moonflower's branching vines. You absolutely *had* to gaze at the Moonflower. The more I gazed, the more it dumbfounded me.

NOTE BY VERITY: *For once, doesn't Timmy sound tongue-tied? But the Moonflower WAS a dumbfounding thing, of course. All I could see at the time, though, was a shimmer of silver light. Lew had told me that the Moonflower was a climber, a member of the morning glory family, only gigantic. It had grown there since anyone could remember. It had wrapped its vines around the peak of the mountain and had sunk its roots clear down to the mountain's floor.*

Imagine. On the very top of the mountain, there was this towerlike formation of rock. And the Moonflower had twined all around it, every vine as thick as the trunk of an oak. Dark leaves like heart-shaped platters grew on it, and thousands of blossoms like huge silver bells. The blossoms were closed now, their heads hanging, but still they gave off a clear silver light. They made the whole room under the dome as bright as noon.

When they opened, I guessed, each blossom would be as big around as a marching-band's tuba and probably dazzling. But their smell! Most perfume makes me gag, but not the Moonflower's. It made me want to sing, even though I can't.

Huge as that round dome was, it wasn't big enough. The blossoms were pressing against its black glass ceiling, getting crushed. The great vines seemed to be writhing around, while the blossoms rustled and whispered, *No room to bloom...under the dome!* And then again, softly, more yearningly—*Room to bloom! Oh, for room...room to bloom!*

"Makes you almost cry just to listen to 'em," said my grandmother with a sigh. The dove made a low moan of sympathy. "It's that Raoul," muttered Gran. She dashed her empty watering bucket to the ground and kicked it with the toe of her boot. I guessed she wished the old bucket was the Dictator's rear section.

"He's trying to kill it," she said grimly, seating herself on a full paint gallon. "He'd have killed it long ago, no doubt, but he doesn't dare come near it. Nor his owls, either."

A giggle got away from me. Gran whirled, her eyes popping even wider. She peered all around, but couldn't see anything. Finally, she sighed and went back to thinking out loud.

"And why," she asked the dove, "is Raoul afraid of the Moonflower? Can't he stand anything beautiful? Works of art. Birds. Animals. People, beautiful people. If only I could see my twins again! And Agamemnon Duff—is he still down in that dreadful mine? Oh, what's the use? I'll be trapped here under this dome forever. I'll never see a one of them again!"

Well, I couldn't stand to hear her go on like that. It seemed high time to unhide. Quiet as a mouse, I tiptoed up to her, till I could have reached out and touched her, and said, "What do you mean you aren't going to see us again?"

With a shriek, Gran leaped to her feet. "Who said that? Who's there?"

"It's me, Gran!" I shouted. "Don't you know me? I'm Timothy, and Verity's here too!" Unable to hold myself back any longer, I grabbed her and gave her a huge hug.

But the effect on my grandmother wasn't what I'd expected. She screeched and staggered backwards, fighting me off. Now she was booting at me, missing me, booting at the air.

"You're a ghost!" she cried. "I'm hearing things! Feeling things! I'm off my rocker! They've kept me under this dismal dome too long!"

"No, Gran, no!" yelped my sister, right beside me, "it's really us, Timmy and me! Look, look at us!"

"No!" said my grandmother firmly, clapping a hand across her eyes. "I won't look. My lonesome old head is playing tricks on me!"

I felt sorry, now, that we had been so sneaky. Gran wouldn't be reassured. She had hold of her paint bucket by its handle and she was swinging the thing like a bomb she was going to hurl.

"One step closer, you ghosts," she threatened, her eyes clamped shut, "and I'm braining you!"

She would have done it, too, if Verity hadn't kept talking to her, calming her down, until at last Gran opened her eyes and said, "Timothy? Verity? Is it you?"

Soon the three of us were trading hugs, and Gran was half crying and half laughing all together. She really had believed that Verity and I were ghosts. The lying baroness, just to torment her, had told her we had both caught our deaths of cold down in the mine.

"My twins!" said Gran, her eyes shining. You ARE my twins! I can't believe it! Why, Timothy, Verity—children, how you've grown!"

"Yeah, that's right, Mrs. Duff," put in Lew from my collar, "they've grown—in lots of ways. The boy kid, especially. He's a little braver than he used to be."

"Wonderful!" Gran cried, on hearing how we'd made our way to Other Earth. "To step through a river! To fight stone owls! Why, what has become of my dear old timid Timothy? Oh, but—my stars! You could have been hurt!"

Suddenly she was staring behind me. "EEEEK! What ever is *that?*" On all fours, the brown bear had come shambling to us, and now he had reared up on his hind feet.

"Don't be scared, Gran," I said quickly. And when I told her how Fardels had defended us, Gran folded him into another of her famous hugs. When we introduced Mustard to her, Gran looked at him sharply and said, "Young man, there's something familiar about you. Haven't we met before?"

The mustard-haired kid shot her a grin. "No, Ma'am, not that I know of. But I wish I had met you long ago."

All seated on the ground in a circle around Gran's paint-bucket chair, we divided a box of soda crackers—Gran's food rations. Lew, the lucky stiff, took off for the vines of the Moonflower and soon he was gorging on aphids. Shelley, with a boost from Verity, fixed himself on a gigantic Moonflower leaf, where he soaked up a supper of juice.

Forced to live under that grim black dome and eat just soda crackers and sleep on a moldy old rug, Gran had managed, in her clever way, to make the place fit for a queen. She had collected small beautiful items: a lump of quartz, a few bright feathers. Floating in a paint bucket were some silver petals dropped from the Moonflower. Gran even had a water-soaked copy of Gramp's book, *The Light to Live By*, brought along inside her pocket from our Earth. During her stay under the dome she had painted a lot of new pictures, using brushes twisted together from fur and twine that the windmill moths had gathered for her. She had done portraits—from memory—of Verity and me and Gramp. All were painted in black, the only color she had available.

Most of the painting she did, we soon saw, was of a different kind. All of a sudden, from a loudspeaker, a mechanical voice roared: "Prisoner Four-seven-three-four!"

"Oh-oh," Gran said to us. "More work for me."

"You are resting, prisoner," accused the voice of an owl. "Moonflower light is escaping from section nine-thirteen of the dome. Correct this at once. Moonflower light must not escape. Reply!"

"Yes, yes, I'll see to it," Gran called wearily, reaching for her paint bucket and a house-painter's brush. Parking a ladder against a wall of the dome that said 913, she climbed to a section of glass where the paint looked worn, and she hit it a swipe with her brush. That must have stopped the escaping light, because the loudspeaker quit barking at her.

"That's my job," said Gran, rejoining us. "To keep on painting all the time. You see, the Moonflower's light is powerful. It keeps wearing the color off the dome, and Raoul doesn't want that happening."

"But Gran," said Verity, "aren't you better at landscapes?"

"That's what I told Raoul Owlstone, but do you think he cared? No—I was *some* kind of painter, that's all that mattered, he had work for me. Now, Raoul doesn't know it, but I help out the Moonflower. Every night I scrape away some of the paint and let a patch of moonlight shine in on the flower. That feeds it. Then in the morning, I cover up the scrape with paint again."

All the while we talked, the restless Moonflower kept stirring. One of its thick green vines cruised down and stroked me on the cheek, gently, like the trunk of some shy, inquisitive elephant. Then it drew back.

"It approves you, Timothy," Gran said with a smile. "You see, right now is when the blossoms try to come out for the night. They know when evening is near, even with this dreadful bowl on top of them. The plant wakes up and stirs and twists, looking for room to bloom. It keeps searching for more moonlight and not finding any. And so nowadays it just sleeps day and night. This dome! Oh, I wish I could smash it to smithereens!"

Just then a feeble scratching made me turn. A weak-looking windmill moth came squeezing in through the gap under the edge of the dome, its wings going around, but just barely.

"Any—juice?" it begged in a frail voice.

Gran helped the moth over to a blossom and pried open the petals for it. The starved moth uncurled a long tongue, like one of those paper favors you blow out at a birthday party. Soon it gave a grateful *Aaaahh-hh-hh!* and, much revived, went churning away, its wings working like speedy paddlewheels. By now, if it hadn't been for Gran, the last of the moths—and the Moonflower— would have been goners.

By the time we ran out of talk, the night was half through. Soon it would be Raoul's coronation day. We laid plans. With Fardels to fight and Lew to scout, the three of us kids would creep up on Raoul and the baroness and somehow overpower them. Slim as our chances might be, we had to try. But right now, feeling pretty tired, we stretched out for a nap on the warm ground, while Gran and the mourning dove and the Moonflower watched over us.

When we were ready to leave the dome, Gran took a necklace from around her own neck and she hung it around Verity's. She kissed Verity and said, "Child, wear this for me. It's only a simple thing I made. I want to give you something."

Even though the necklace was nothing fancy— it was only a piece of string painted black—its pendant was something special. It was a Moonflower seed, an oblong thing like an almond that gave off a clear silver glow.

Then Gran kissed me, too, and she told me to take care of myself and Verity. We promised her that as soon as we had captured Raoul and Ratisha we'd be back for her.

Fardels was the first to depart. The brown bear had a hard time wriggling his bulk out through the gap. Mustard followed, then Verity, with the snail in her back pocket. Then, with Lew on my collar, I crawled out last.

As I inched my way through the space under the thick glass wall—a distance of maybe a yard— I was humming with hopes. Seeing Gran and the Moonflower had cheered me mightily. Today was a whole new day. We were going to show Raoul Owlstone a thing or two!

But when I emerged into the glum dawn of the mountainside, I was in for a shock.

A gang of tall owls had been waiting for us. They'd already surrounded the bear and Mustard and Verity, and now they closed in on me and Lew.

From out of the fog a large round bubble swam. It drew closer, and I saw it was a man.

"Well, well, well," said Raoul Owlstone. "It was worth getting up early this morning to win a few prizes like YOU. The dome is alive with hidden microphones. My owls heard everything you said."

On the Dictator's shoulder, a batlike shape stood up and fluffed itself. Its shrill cry rang down the mountainside:

"Eat them! Eat! Eat meat!"

16. *Who Cracked the Lock?*

Was the dungeon of Owlstone Hall ever *cold!* You could just about hear the tinkling of your breath. The owls had flung us into a cell and slammed the bars, and they'd snapped a padlock to keep us there. Our luck, it now seemed, had hit bottom. And my sister was throwing a temper fit.

"Dimwits! That's us!" she yelled, stamping on the owlstone floor. "Now tonight, Raoul will crown himself Emperor and kill everybody! While we sit here like a bundle of dopes!"

Nobody was in a mood to argue with her. Fardels, quietly growling to himself, was slumped in one corner of our jail cell, uselessly cleaning his claws. Lew clung like a button to my collar, saying nothing. Even Mustard had run out of his usual cheer.

That cell wasn't long on furniture. All it held was a bench too short to stretch out on and, for drinking water, a bucket of sea-green slime. To warm up, I paced the cell, reading comments that prisoners before us had scratched into the walls—things like RATISHA IS A MUCK PILL and STAMP OUT STONE OWLS. When I had run out of reading matter, I went over to the one window-slot we had. From out of it, you could stare down a quarter-mile to the floor of the valley. Below me sat the abandoned zoo, with its vacant cages and its forgotten popcorn stand. Already, the tops of the trees were turning a muck-colored brown. Summer ought to last longer, but the fall now hurried on. No doubt the season was changing early because Raoul's factory smoke had shut off the warmth of the sun. Muckhawks, shrieking taunts, glided past me.

"So what now, Lew?" I asked the red dot on my collar. No answer. Worried, I hollered his name.

"Huh? What?" said the ladybug, waking. "Oh. Sorry, kid—cold weather makes me sleepy. If it gets any colder than this, I'll have to go look up my cousins on the mountaintop. Our whole family gets together every winter for a slumber party." He yawned.

"NO!" howled my sister. "Lew, you can't leave us now! This is the day of Raoul's coronation! He has to be stopped!"

"Raoul?" the detective said blankly. "Raoul who? Oh, yeah—I remember him. You'll have to excuse me, beautiful, I'm a little bit thick in the bean. Can I come sit on your Moonflower seed a minute? It looks warm."

And shaking himself, the detective went wobbling through the air and landed on Verity's pendant. Where it hung from its string, the seed gave a silvery glow. Lew sat on it and rubbed his forefeet together like someone warming himself in front of a fire.

Fardels gave a yawn like the roar of a lion. "Sleepy—that's how I feel. When there's frost in the air, I look for a nice warm cave." He yawned again. "Maybe I'll just go to sleep right here. Wake me up when it's April, all right?"

Grabbing the bear around the shoulders, I tried hard to give him a shake. His dreamy eyes were starting to cross.

"Come on, Fardels," said Mustard, doing some fancy footwork in front of him, "put up your paws and let's go a few rounds."

Fardels struggled to his hind feet. The kid was throwing punches at him. "Yeah," said the bear, "let's spar. Help me keep my eyes open. Come on. Mix it up." He and Mustard went through the motions of a clumsy boxing match, with nobody landing any blows.

The warmth of the seed had brought Lew back to life. "Wouldn't you know," he rasped, "that's just what the doctor ordered. Think I'll take a spin around the Hall and see what's up." And he skimmed out between our cell-door bars and vanished down the corridor like a dart.

All morning long, as I stared out into the gloomy passageway, stone owls kept rumbling by. None of them gave us a glance. "Hey, jailer!" I yelled. "Don't we get fed today?"

An owl with a chip out of its head came tooling over. No, Raoul had not ordered any food for us, so we would not be given any.

That was one thing I liked about owls. They would answer all questions put to them.

"Why," I asked through the bars, "are you owls so busy this morning?"

"Dictator Owlstone will be crowned Emperor this evening," the machine-voice droned. "We prepare the celebration."

"Well, I don't see how Raoul can be coronated. Dr. Weedblossom can't have finished the owlstone crown."

"The owlstone crown is finished. Dictator Owlstone could not wait. He had Dr. Weedblossom sent to the mine. He finished the crown himself."

Then the inventor hadn't been able to stall! Mustard, at this news, groaned hard and clenched his fists.

This owl was full of answers. Just for fun, I asked, "Listen, owl, what's the secret of Owlstone Hall?"

A whirring and clicking came from the owl's stone head as it searched its memory. Finally it droned, "That information is not in my supply."

Oh well. No harm asking.

"Who bopped you on the head?" I wanted to know. "How come there's a chunk of you missing?"

"A woman named Maw Grimble. She hit me with a metallic object called a potato masher."

For Pete's sake! I was flabbergasted! From the back of the cell my sister called, "Really, owl? Then you must be the same owl Timmy shoved into the river, am I right?"

The dumb dodo! Now why did she have to go and remind a dangerous owl of that? But the owl just flashed its eye-cells and droned, "Assumption is correct."

"Then tell me, owl," I persisted, "when Maw Grimble bopped you, what did you do?"

"I deposited her and her mate into a pen with their dog called Rouser. I then returned to Other Ear-rr-rr-r—*awwwk-kk!*—*squawwk-k-k!*"

The owl made a noise like a garbage truck with a bottle stuck in its lifter. This was because another owl, a tall boss, had rolled up behind it and ordered, "Stop talking to prisoners. You will remove your violin from storage and report to the Grand Ballroom."

Our informer had to turn and roll away.

"Now why," said Mustard after the owls had gone, "why do you suppose Raoul wants an owl to play the violin?"

"I can tell you," said the detective, sitting back down on my collar. "Raoul and the baroness are throwing a party tonight. It's going to be a swell affair—so they claim. They've invited all the Elders from all over the country. They're going to have music and dancing and sandwiches."

"What? Raoul and Ratisha giving a party?" Fardels looked surprised. "Since when did those two stingy birds ever *give* anybody anything?"

"Oh, they're giving away plenty tonight," said the detective sourly. "They're going to give away doses of poison. Verity got a whiff of the stuff when the baroness was boiling it. Those Elders' lives aren't worth a plugged nickel."

"Lew," I said, "Lew, how can we warn them?"

"Too late, junior—the invites went out days ago. Any minute now, all the Elders should be starting to arrive."

I was miserable. But just then, a fresh worry came along. From deep in the core of the mountain, there was a long, low muttering. Suddenly the floor of the cell shuddered under our feet. Our bucket of slime tipped over. For a minute I hoped the walls would split open and set us free. But the muttering stopped as quickly as it had begun.

"What was that?" growled the bear.

"Only a little earthquake," said Lew. "Probably just a few timbers falling, down in the mine."

"A mine cave-in? Oh, no!" shrilled my sister.

"Gramp and all those miners are still down there!"

"Sorry, beautiful," said the ladybug. "I didn't mean to throw you any scare. But there's something funny going on inside this mountain. Just what, I only wish I knew."

The mysterious tremor had left us edgy and nervous. And Fardels kept looking sleepier all the time.

Day wore on, and the light—what could squeeze through our window-slot—inched slowly around to the west. Soon it would be Coronation Night.

From high above us, from the Hall's Grand Ballroom, faint music drifted. Well, something like music. We could hear the woody squawk of clarinets, the scrape of fiddles, a tuba's deep syrupy burp. The orchestra of owls was tuning up.

"Sis, what'll we do?" I pleaded with Verity. In the past, she had always told me.

"Timmy," she said, shaking her head, "we can't do anything. Raoul and Ratisha are going to poison all the Elders. Raoul is going to rule forevermore. It'll happen. Shelley predicted it would."

All this while, the snail had been napping in her back pocket. Now, hearing its name, it poked its tiny horns out over the pocket's rim. "I. Am. Sorry. To. Foresee. Such. A. Future," it apologized.

I sighed. "Aw, Shelley, the future's not your fault. What about *our* future? Have we got any?"

In Verity's cupped hand, the snail retreated into its chambers. We waited and watched. What was it doing in there? What movie of things to come was being projected on its walls? What did it hear from the slosh of invisible tides?

At last, its horns came back out, quivering. A high small faraway voice said:

Stone. Owls. Do. Not. A. Prison. Make.

Nor. Owlstone. Bars. A. Cage.

"Huh?" said Lew. "What does that prove? Isn't there anything more?"

But the prophet had spoken. Verity thanked it and put it back into her pocket. Now she was leaning against the floor-to-ceiling bars of our cell door, her dim eyes staring hopelessly down the corridor.

Mustard decided he'd test the prophecy, slamming himself against the thick stone bars of the door, dropping back. He just bopped his head uselessly. "These bars sure make a cage, if you ask me."

"It's no use," I said glumly, "we won't get out of here in a million y—"

My words quit, because my jaw had fallen. To my amazement, the round stone padlock on the bars was springing a leak.

I bounded to Verity's side and blinked at it. Out of its keyhole a fast stream of dirty water was trickling. In front of my eyes, the whole lock was dwindling like a snowball in July. A second later it turned to slush and it dropped with a *ploop!* to the floor.

"Well I'll be a monkey's uncle," said Lew Ladybug.

"The lock's been cracked!" Mustard trumpeted. "Who did it? Who cracked the lock?"

"It wasn't me," said Verity in puzzlement.

"What do we care who cracked it?" bellowed Fardels, suddenly wide awake. "The bars are melting too! Let's get out of here!"

The bear was right. As we watched, the floor-to-ceiling bars of the door grew thinner and thinner. Fardels shoved a paw against them and they tinkled to the floor, leaving a hole—which we quickly stepped out through.

But our jailer, the tall owl, had heard us. Speeding down the corridor it came, its beak darting underneath a wing, searching for its cone-shaped radio to sound an alarm.

Not able to see where she was going, Verity had stepped right into the jailer's path. The tall owl rumbled down on her and she bumped into it. Thrown off balance, the owl leaned forward on its ball-bearing, almost touching her.

"Sis, get away from that owl!" I yelled.

But then, in the gray stone chest of our jailer, a black hole opened. A hole as big around as a basketball. Just like the bars and the padlock, the owl was melting. I watched its body twist around on top of its rolling ball. Then its head collapsed, and the rest of its body trickled down into a puddle of slush. A mess of ice, fog, muck, and polluted water. The owl had gone back to its elements.

"Timmy, what's happening?" my sister wanted to know.

I started to tell her—and then it hit me. Hit me like a meteor.

The secret of Owlstone Hall.

I said, "Listen, everybody. I've got a plan..."

I talked fast, and when I'd finished, Lew looked at me with glee in his compound eyes. "Right as rain, kid," he said, "that's the secret, all right. Your plan is about as likely to succeed as a pig is likely to sing opera. But it may be our only chance."

My plan split us up into two bunches. Bunch One—Verity and the snail, Lew and I—would try to enter the ballroom. Mustard gave me the clasped little-finger handshake. Then we set off, Mustard commanding Bunch Two, the powerful brown bear loping at his side.

17. *The Crown Descends*

A night with no moon. Gray fog, filmy as tissue paper, surrounded Owlstone Hall, making the giant toadstool look like a gift that had been wrapped carelessly. In the stem of the Hall, the big front doors had been flung open, letting the hoots and squawks of the orchestra drift outside.

We had all made our way out of the dungeon. As mysteriously as the lock had melted, and the jailer owl, a hole had gaped in a wall for us to step out through. Now Bunch One—Verity and Shelley, Lew and I—were outside, crouched behind a screen of bushes, where we could watch the Hall's front doors.

Raoul and Ratisha stood in the doorway greeting the Elders. The baroness had on a long black dress that made her look as if she'd been dipped in ink. Raoul, in a purple tuxedo, looked shiny and round as an eggplant that's all set to rot. On his right shoulder, Chuckles, his pet muckhawk, littered the night with screams.

In a parking lot in front of the Hall, the Elders were pulling up in their horse-drawn buggies. The Elders were a white-haired lot—some women, some men—and they walked with dignity. Suddenly Lew, on my collar, gave a whistle. "Here comes the biggest shot of all."

Clipping and clopping along the driveway came the buggy of someone important. He had *two* white horses pulling him, with a driver for each. Right away, Lew knew him: Aspen Appleyard, the eldest Elder.

"Are we close enough?" one of the horses inquired, turning his head to his driver. The buggy halted in front of us.

Twittering, Lew darted into the air. "Elder Appleyard!" he shrilled.

Out of the buggy's window poked a head without hair. A wrinkled, leathery face inspected us, and a kind voice said, "Why, Lew Ladybug. What can I do for you?"

"Plenty," said the detective, touching down on the buggy's windowsill. "You're risking your life to come here, do you know that?"

"Just as I thought," said the eldest Elder with a sigh. "And suppose I'd refused to come? No doubt an owl would have dragged me. Well, Lew, have you investigated? What does Raoul plan for us?"

"Sudden death. So don't eat anything. Don't drink anything. Just close your trap."

Then Lew introduced Verity and me to Appleyard, and he said I had a plan. He asked the Elder if he knew any way to smuggle us into the ballroom.

Appleyard pondered. Then his face lit into a grin. "They'll be my gift-bearers," he said, and he skimmed the hats from the heads of his two drivers—three-cornered hats, like what George Washington's soldiers wore—and he clapped them on me and Verity. The hats were too big. Mine slumped to my nose.

"You see," Appleyard went on, "every guest was told to bring Raoul a gift tonight. We weren't told why. Now, me, I've brought a crate of eating apples. You two children look good and strong— you can carry it. Keep your hats pulled down, and maybe Raoul won't notice you."

Oh-oh. This would be a pretty thin disguise! I felt a sudden chill, not just from the night. Lew took off to go scout the ballroom, saying he'd meet us inside. With the help of Appleyard's drivers, Verity and I boosted the crate up onto our shoulders. It must have weighed half a ton.

NOTE BY VERITY: *Exaggerating. Always exaggerating. The crate didn't weigh more than thirty pounds, if that much.*

Keeping our heads lowered, marching side by side in back of Appleyard, we approached the front steps of the Hall. Dry leaves crackled under our feet.

"Go slow, Timmy!" my sister whispered. "I can't see, you know!"

"Well I can't, either," I told the inside of my hat.

At the foot of the steps, an owl crossed Appleyard's name off a list. It droned, "Ascend and be greeted by their Vilenesses."

Up the steps we went. Panting under the weight of our cargo, we marched—with me quaking in my shoes—straight up to Raoul and the baroness.

"I'm here," I heard Appleyard say grimly.

"So you are," said the Dictator. "And what's this present you've brought?"

He was looking at our burden! I quaked harder. What if he recognized us? But luckily, Raoul had eyes only for the present. He didn't bother to check the faces under it.

"It's apples," said the Elder. "The best I can grow these days. Hard and green and riddled with worms. Rotten spots in 'em."

"Never mind," Raoul hooted. "I can bite around those. All right, old man, don't stand here blocking the doorway all night. Into the Hall with you!"

Verity shot at me under her breath, "Oh, the big lunk! I'd like to give him a karate chop!"

"Wait!" broke in the thin sharp voice of the baroness. "You—you bearer who just whispered! I know your voice. Have we not met?"

Holy smoke! I suddenly longed for a canyon to open up under me. I expected my sister to answer, "Sure, you know me—I'm the girl who used to scrub your pots."

But Verity just kept her head bent. "Met?" she murmured. "Oh, yes, we must have met *somewhere*. Let's go, brother!"

From behind us, another Elder, a gabby one, bounced forward and grabbed the baroness by the hand and said how much he'd been wanting to meet her. Before Ratisha could think twice, the two of us and our apple crate swept past her into the Hall.

"Well done," Appleyard said admiringly. "But—whew! That one was close!"

The Grand Ballroom, as it turned out, was the same big room where we'd first seen Raoul and Ratisha breakfasting. A few extra candles had been added, but the place was still dim as the inside of a tomb. The table, a hundred feet long, now overflowed with presents, and we added our rotten apples to its pile. An owlstone vase held a couple of table flowers—the kind that trapped and digested flies.

Tall owls, in gold-roped uniforms, lined every wall. There was music, but no one was dancing. The owl fiddlers—I recognized our friend with the dented head—were sawing mechanically. That orchestra could barely carry a tune, although I managed to make out "The Funeral

March" and "The Worms Crawl In, the Worms Crawl Out." Somehow, in that dismal cold gray ballroom, that music sounded absolutely right.

My tumbledown hat kept me looking at the floor, and there I got a sudden shock. At my feet—in the middle of the room—lay the familiar oval form of a small pond.

"*Cressida!*" I wailed. "What's happened to you?"

I flung myself down beside her. The water woman didn't sparkle any longer. Her waters now looked thick and green and full of soggy cigarette butts. As I stared, a rainbow trout—Fiona, I guessed—made a tired leap out of the pond and sank back again.

Now Verity, too, was kneeling on the floor beside me, and Shelley, who had once lived in the pond, poked its horns out of Verity's pocket and said, "Oh. No. —Don't. Die. Beautiful. Mistress."

Dimly, the water woman tried to shape her face. It looked vague and blurry and wavering. Cressida tried to thrust out a hand to us, but she couldn't quite form her fingers.

"Is that—you—Timothy Tibb—Verity?" she whispered.

"Cressida," I said urgently, "we'll get you out of here."

Her faint lips made slow ripples. "Don't let them—catch you—as they—caught me!"

"How did they catch you, Cressida?"

"The owls heard—that I—befriended you.

They—brought me here—in an egg."

By my side, Verity was weeping bitterly.

"Be careful," the liquid voice trickled. "Raoul—is planning—something terrible..."

Then her eyes clouded over. Her face seemed to sink and withdraw from us.

"Sis, this is awful!" I said. "Cressida is in a bad way. She looks as if Raoul has been using her for an ashtray, or something."

"Watch out, Timmy—I hear high heels coming!"

It was the baroness. She had been circling the room, making talk to people, and now, still suspicious of Verity and me, she came over to our side of the pond, clicking her ballroom shoes.

"Admiring the birdbath, are you?" she purred. "Raoul's muckhawk often takes dips in it."

Verity kept her hat lowered, but she answered, "Yes—it's the only thing of yours that we admire."

I could just imagine Ratisha squinting through her monocle. "I beg your pardon?" she said as if annoyed.

"She means," I quickly piped through my hat, "it's what we MOST admire."

"So glad you do," said the baroness absently. No doubt her eyes were roaming the room, looking for somebody more interesting to talk to than a couple of apple-luggers. Soon, to my relief, she murmured and was gone.

Raoul Owlstone, too, was touring the crowd. When he came to us, he snarled, "You cheap flunkies, those apples you brought me taste terrible. Don't swill too much of my lemonade."

Cringing deeper into my hat, I made him a bow.

Lew landed on my collar. "Just like you'd expect," he rasped. "It's to be a wholesale poisoning. I can't figure, though, how they plan to give out the poison. Nobody's keeled over yet, so it can't be in the lemonade. But something bad is supposed to happen at nine o'clock."

Out of the crowd swam another face we knew— Mustard's mother, Mrs. Weedblossom. Just as she'd hoped, she had found work as a waitress in the Hall. Wearing a short black dress and a wrinkly white starched cap, she had been going around the ballroom, a pitcher in her hand, refilling glasses with lemonade—the cheap kind made with powder and water. When she laid her green-and-brown eyes on us, she came right over and tossed me a smile that warmed me all over. "Aren't you the boy I met on the bridge?" she asked.

"Hello," I said.

"And who is your friend under the other hat?"

"Shhh-hh!" I warned, "don't give us away, please. That's only my sister. We're spying."

"How can I help?"

Lew raised a rasp from my collar. "Keep your ears unlatched, Mrs. Weedblossom, will you? Find out how they're going to slip the poison to every-body."

"Poison? Don't tell me!" The friendly woman's two-colored eyes looked ready to pop. But just then came a new disturbance from down inside the mountain. Under our feet a rumbling grew, like a giant clearing his throat. A chandelier over our heads started to sway. Next to where I stood by the gifts table, a shudder ran down a wall. People were screaming and yelling, "Oh! Oh!"

"It's an earthquake!"

"We're doomed!"

"Quiet!" bellowed the Dictator. "Maybe you're doomed, all right, but not by a quake. It's nothing but a little rumble down in the mine. This mountain is honeycombed with tunnels. They're all the time caving in on somebody. Don't give it a thought—we've plenty of miners to spare! Drink your lemonade! Play, owls, play!"

The fiddlers grabbed their bows in their beaks and began to assassinate a waltz. With a glance that promised to help us, Mrs. Weedblossom went on with her rounds.

My sister was growing anxious. "Timmy, is Raoul really going to be Emperor? Well, is he?"

"How should I know?" I said with a groan. "Oh, what in heck is keeping Mustard and Fardels?"

A grandfather clock in one corner of the ball-room kept on ticking—ticking faster than I liked.

Now all of a sudden it spoke with a slow, solemn chime—

CLUNNGG-GG-G-G-G!

Raoul, in the middle of the room, gave a hoot of glee. "One minute to nine!" With a sweep of one fat hand he shut off the orchestra.

"Now listen, all of you," he said commandingly. "I suppose you wonder why I've asked you here tonight. Well, it isn't because I like you. I'm sick and tired of you yapping Elders, always complaining about the way I run things. So I've asked you here to watch a little ceremony. I'm not going to be just your Dictator any more. When the clock strikes nine I'll crown myself Emperor. Emperor of Owlstonia!" The muckhawk on his shoulder screamed happily.

A giant gasp went rippling through the crowd. Someone cried, "Emperor? Owlstonia? Never!"

"Why should you be Emperor?" cried somebody else. "This is the Land of the Moonflower. Why change the name to Owlstonia?"

"Because I want to be Emperor," said Raoul. "Because soon there won't be a Moonflower anymore." He stood there rocking on his heels, a satisfied smirk on his face.

CLUNNGG-G-G! went the clock, for the second time.

Aspen Appleyard was striding forward, shaking a fist at the Dictator. "Raoul Owlstone, we've had enough of you! I don't know why we ever made you Dictator. Your baroness must have bewitched us. But you won't become Emperor! We won't stand for it!"

Raoul's little owl-eyes shrank to pinpoints. "Appleyard, you're a troublemaker. I'll soon settle you."

CLUNGG-G-G-G-G!

The hollow sound vibrated through the ballroom, shaking the owlstone walls. Four tall owls rolled into the room, each holding the corner of a cushion in its beak. In the middle of the cushion, a huge gray object squatted. It was studded with tall spears and cat's eye jewels. The owlstone crown.

At the sight of this menacing thing, Raoul was oozing happiness. "Clean out your ears, all of you! When the clock strikes the hour, I'll be Emperor—and all you Elders will be nobodies!"

CLUNG!—CLUNG!—CLUNG-G-G!—

"For crying out loud!" Lew rasped from my collar, "where in the Sam Hill are Mustard and the bear?"

CLUNG-G-G-G!

Now the Elders were going wild. Yelling and bawling, they made desperate grabs at the Dictator—but tall owls wheeled out from the walls and slung them away.

CLUNG-G-G!—

"Oh, I've got butterflies inside me," said Raoul

nervously. "I don't get to be Emperor every day!"

The ninth note of the clock echoed through the gloom, a long wobbling CLUNG-GG-GG-GG! that died in a hideous CLUNK.

Nine o'clock in Owlstonia.

We had lost.

"What are you waiting for, Raoul, you ninny?" the baroness jeered. "Take that crown and set it on your head!"

"All right. Don't rush me—I want to enjoy myself. Owls, give me the crown!"

Inside me, I felt as if a hard, cold sleet was falling. To think that I knew Raoul's secret—the secret of Owlstone Hall! And it didn't do the slightest bit of good!

Raoul was holding the crown in both hands, looking at it the way a hungry man studies a T-bone steak. With a grunt and a heave, he hoisted the great weight of stone and set it down squarely on his head.

A groan as tall as a tidal wave rolled through the room. The muckhawk, which had been fluttering in the air, settled down on the shoulder of the new Emperor.

"Has he done it?" asked my sister, ready to cry. "Has he crowned himself?"

I put my arm around her. I gulped down my own tears.

18. *The Flight of the Hawk*

The crown jabbed the air with its owlstone spears. Its snakeskin cap was glittering. Its jewels shone green-and-yellow, like cats' eyes.

From under it, Emperor Raoul the First gave a booming laugh. "We're going to celebrate! Elders, you'll all get some freshly made sandwiches. This waitress"—he pointed to Mrs. Weedblossom—"will pass among you with a tray of them. Make sure you each take one and chew it good, or you'll insult my hospitality."

"What?" cried Aspen Appleyard. "Only one tray of sandwiches for this crowd?"

"Don't worry, Your Eldership," said the baroness coldly. "There'll be enough to take care of you."

"So that's their plan!" shrilled Lew. "The poison's in the sandwiches! Let's warn everybody. I'll tell Mrs. Weedblossom. You kids help spread the word!"

"Eat! Eat!" shrieked the muckhawk on Raoul's shoulder, and the Emperor hooted, "That's right, eat, eat, everybody! Lobster salad! Lettuce and tomato! Enjoy!"

Verity and I scurried around the ballroom together, hissing to everybody, "The sandwiches— don't eat the sandwiches!" And you can imagine how flabbergasted those Elders were, to have a ladybug suddenly twitter into their ears, "One bite of that sandwich, kiddo, and it's your last."

Raoul kept urging the crowd to dig in, and yet Mrs. Weedblossom's tray, I was happy to see, stayed piled high. But when the waitress came to one crusty old fellow —Elder Elm Elderberry— she met trouble. While she was warning him, the Elder's face went red as a beet.

"See here, Owlstone," he stormed, "what's the meaning of this? Your waitress offers me a sandwich, and she tells me that if I taste it I'll die."

"Guards!" snarled the Emperor, "arrest her!" Two tall owls rolled out and fenced in Mrs. Weedblossom. With a flourish, the baroness swept the tray from the woman's hands and offered it to Elm Elderberry.

"Go ahead, Your Eldership," she purred. "Try the lobster salad."

"Don't mind if I do," said the Elder haughtily.

Just as the old fellow was going to bite into a mouthwatering poison-on-rye, a commotion broke out. Chuckles the muckhawk had leaped from the Emperor's shoulder. With a squawk and a thrash, the greedy bird swooped down and ripped the sandwich right out of Elderberry's hand.

"Crook!" shouted the Elder in a rage.

Under his crown, Raoul's smile fell apart like a melting popsicle. "Chuckles, baby! Don't swallow that! Spit out that sandwich, quick, before it's too late!"

"Do you mean to say," thundered Elderberry, "that a sandwich fit for an Elder isn't fit for a muckhawk?"

The baroness quickly rustled to his side. "No, no, Your Eldership, calm yourself. Of course there's nothing wrong with the sandwich. It is simply that lobster and muckhawks do not agree."

Perched on the chandelier, Chuckles Baby uttered a sickening burp. His snake-eyes crossed, and he began to croak horribly. Then he took off. Like a runaway comet, he started to roar around and around the ballroom, while everybody dived to the floor.

"Shoot him down!" hooted the Emperor. A guard with a pistol in its beak shot off a splatter of muck. It missed the whooshing bird, but it muddied a few of the guests.

What happened next was pretty awful. As Chuckles was making another circle around the ballroom, he let out one ear-splitting scream. From beak to tail, the muckhawk stiffened—right there

in the middle of the air. Swooping down, down, down in a lazy glide, his dead body went skimming out through one of the room's look-out slots and dived for the swallowing valley.

"Good riddance," grunted Lew.

"Eh!" cried Elderberry in amazement. "If that's what the lobster sandwiches do, I'll try the salami."

"No, don't, Your Eldership," sang out Mrs. Weedblossom from between her guards, "the salami can kill you, too!"

"Elderberry," said the Emperor, "you're a slow eater."

"And what if I had gobbled down that sandwich?" the Elder retorted. "Would I—just like that dirty bird—have gone whizzing around the room and out the window?"

"Owlstone," roared Appleyard, "I accuse you! You are trying to poison us all!"

"So you know," the Emperor said bitterly. "All right, it's true. I invited you stuffed shirts here only to wipe you out."

A gasp of horror came from the crowd.

"Monster!" shrieked a woman Elder. "Call my horse and buggy—I am leaving immediately!"

"Oh no, you're not," the Emperor glowered. "Nobody's leaving. One move out of any of you and I'll blast you to a blot."

In Raoul's hand, something black and stubby glittered. It wasn't anything made of owlstone.

Lew whistled from my collar. "He's got a .45!"

Now where in Other Earth could Raoul have found such a weapon? The pistol was deadlier, I knew, than any gun that splattered muck.

"You're first, Appleyard," Raoul said evenly. "Then I'll see about the rest of you. This will be just like shooting fish in a barrel."

His pistol came up and took careful aim at the eldest Elder's head. On the owlstone crown, the green-and-yellow jewels glittered like the eyes of dangerous cats.

I stood next to the table where our crate of apples lay. I didn't really think—there wasn't time—I just grabbed apples and I flung them with all my might at Emperor Raoul.

I never was much of a pitcher. Three or four of my fast balls went wild. But the last one scored. The apple—a really rotten item—struck the muzzle of Raoul's pistol with a plop. The Emperor stood there, his mouth open, looking stunned, while the business end of his gun kept dripping applesauce.

I couldn't help laughing like crazy—but then my laugh kind of gurgled to a stop. A tall owl was standing to the left of me. Another stood to Verity's right. From behind us, the baroness stepped up and knocked off our hats.

"Ha! It's *them!* I might have known!" she shrilled.

"You kids again!" Raoul grated, his face turning blue with rage. Slowly and deliberately he wiped off his pistol with a dirty handkerchief. Now the mean little hole in the gun's muzzle was looking me straight in the eye.

From my collar, Lew talked rapidly. "Listen, Owlstone, are you itching for a wooden overcoat? I'm telling you, you hurt one hair of these kids and—"

"So long, bug," Raoul said coldly. "You can take these pestering kids along with you."

Paralyzed, I watched the trigger squeeze. Close by my side, my sister cried my name.

A blast of fire came out of the pistol's throat. Only it didn't touch us—it hit the ceiling. A slim arm of water had flashed out at Raoul's hand. With an effort, Cressida Pond had lifted an arm and swatted the pistol. Now her waterfall voice spoke: "Leave those children alone!"

She flipped the gun into the air and her waters caught it. It splashed in, gurgled, and disappeared.

Behind us, the baroness Ratisha was screeching quietly.

And then it happened.

From outside the Hall came an ear-splitting CRACK-KK-KK!—like something breaking. A sound that must have reached to the mountain's floor. A wave of silver light surged in through the window-slots, flattening the shadows back against the walls.

"Timmy, I can see something!" Verity shouted. "Bright light. REALLY bright. Are they here?"

"They're here, Sis! They've done it!" I capered around and warbled in my joy.

I raced to the nearest window-slot. A beautiful scene was unfolding before my eyes. Up on the mountain, hundreds of miners had circled the base of the Moonflower's huge dome. They were smashing away with picks and shovels, and the hated glass bubble was crumbling in to smithereens. As they worked, they were roaring their happiness. Slabs of glass coasted down the mountainside, and some of them whanged onto the roof of Owlstone Hall. I could see, right in the thick of the fun, Fardels and Mustard and Dr. Weedblossom. The brown bear was smashing away at the dome with a fierce pick. A trim lady— it must have been Gran—was swinging away with a shovel by his side.

In the roof of the giant bubble a jagged crack had opened, and out of it shone a blinding stream of light. As I watched, dazzled, the crack widened, and with a tremendous groan the dome split into halves and those halves rolled slowly aside.

And now, like some immense bird hatching, the Moonflower itself was unfolding, untwisting its cramped vines, climbing the sky. All over the mountaintop, silver blossoms were popping open like a thousand colossal firecrackers on a string. Every time one opened, it gave out a beam brighter than any searchlight's, and it made a chiming sound. The blossoms were alive. They were whispering, *Room to bloom! At last! Some room to bloom!* With a sound like the gong that must have begun Creation, still another blossom was opening—the highest blossom, the biggest one of all. There on the mountain's peak it unfolded its petals, glowing like a kindly bonfire consuming the world.

19. *The Secret of Owlstone Hall*

As the Moonflower opened its blossoms, the Elders were gazing up out of the window-slots of the ballroom, sniffing the rich perfume. They were marveling:

"It's magnificent!"

"Spectacular!"

"Well, I'll be jingoed, I will!"

Being a wrestling champ had helped Verity capture one of the better window-slots. Her upturned face was silvered with Moonflower light. Even *her* eyes could take in that brilliant glow. I waited to hear what she'd say—

"Timmy, something cold is going drip, drip, drip on the back of my neck!"

The drops were slush. They were falling in a steady downpour from the ceiling overhead. I glanced around the room. Wherever the light of the Moonflower was striking, owlstone was starting to melt and drip.

"Ho-ho!" Appleyard chortled, "just look at that stone egg!"

Outside in the air, one of the owlstone copters that circled the Hall was in trouble. It was dissolving like a snowball in the sun. A zigzag crack shot down it, then the whole egg split in two, dumping out several owls who fell, bottom-heavy like raindrops, straight down for a quarter of a mile. Then the halves of the shell spun after them. Seconds later, the other egg cracked open, too, and followed its companion down into the mixing-bowl of the valley.

Just in time, I yanked Verity back from the window-slot before a ton of melted ceiling fell, missing us by inches. Now the whole of the Grand Ballroom was blazing with silvery light. Walls were turning into waterfalls. The ceiling was trickling a steady rain. Cressida Pond had slushy icebergs.

And me, I was hopping with happiness. Things were turning out just the way I'd hoped. The collapse of the dome over the Moonflower had shattered Raoul's greedy dreams. In the middle of the room, the Emperor stood petrified. His crown was dribbling a stream of gray slush down over his brow, and its spikes were bending like wet grass.

"This was your secret, Emperor!" I taunted him. "Moonflower light melts owlstone. Turns it back to what it's made out of — polluted water, ice, fog, muck. You were afraid of a flower, all right—the Moonflower."

Raoul puffed out his chest. "You think I'm finished, do you? Think you won't have Raoul Owlstone to kick around any more? Think again! Didn't the snail make me a prophecy? I'm to rule till the last day of time!"

From Verity's back pocket, Shelley had pricked up its horns. Now, in its shrill, piping voice, it repeated:

Raoul. Shall. Rule. Till. Owlstone. Walls.
Dissolve—

"Yeah," Lew said gleefully, "and now they're dissolving, all right."

"But go on, snail," the Dictator begged in a whining voice. "That wasn't ALL you said!"

And. Raoul. Rule. Till. Moonflower. Mount.
Revolve, the snail finished.

"How about that!" Raoul chortled. "I'm still the boss of this country. And I'm to rule, the snail says, till the mountain turns around. But it isn't ever going to!"

With a look as if she had bitten into a lemon, the baroness was squinting out through a lopsided window-slot. "Raoul," she said worriedly, "I hate to tell you this, but didn't Owlstone Hall always face *west*?"

"Whaa-aa—?" The self-crowned Emperor leaped to the slot, gasped, and staggered backwards as if hit by a football team. "We're facing EAST! I can see the zoo! This is impossible! A mountain can't do an about-face!"

"Sure it can, chubby," the detective grated. "Especially *this* mountain. The Moonflower's roots go deep. Ever since you clapped a dome over it the big plant has been turning every which way looking for room. It must have twisted the mountain around by a hundred and eighty degrees. I'd bet that, because you mined so much muck out of it, you hollowed out the mountain and made it easy to twist."

Verity clapped her hands. "Then that's what all those earthquakes meant! The mountain was starting to revolve!"

The Baroness von Bad Radisch was seething with rage. "How stupid!" she snarled. "Can mere *children*"—she ground out the word with hatred—"stop an army? Destroy an empire? *Children*, one of them blind, and a bear and a snail and a bug?"

"Sure they can." Lew chuckled, enjoying himself. "Now just hand over your pink eyepiece, baby, and tell that fatso next to you to give up, too."

"Surrender?" cried the baroness. "To an insect? Never! Raoul is an Emperor and I—I am a baroness of royal blood!"

Lew took a long time laughing a laugh that wasn't nice to hear. "You can drop that phony baroness stuff with me, Sadie Spittlespoon." He grinned wolfishly. "Yeah, that's right—I know your given name. Oh, I've read the New Jersey State Police blotter on you and your partner. Hugo Pugh, isn't he really called?"

"Great snakes!" exclaimed Elm Elderberry. "Then Ratisha is no more a baroness than my Aunt Tillie's goat?"

"The goat," said the detective coolly, "probably has a lot more class. These two are just a couple of small-time hoods who once ran a crooked massage parlor in Union City. While Sadie here was giving the customers a rubdown, Hugo was rubbing out their wallets and watches. One day the cops gave 'em the chase, and the pair of 'em jumped down a sewer and flowed out to sea. It was our tough luck that there was a full moon, and they fell through a door in the ocean, and landed in this world."

"Don't think I'm a worry-wart," said Verity, "but look down. Isn't the floor dissolving under our feet?"

She was right. Besides, the walls of the ballroom were bulging alarmingly. With a terrible SPLOP! the chandelier let go of the ceiling and shattered all over the floor.

"TIMOTHY! VERITY! ARE YOU ALL RIGHT?"

This shout had come from my grandfather. He

and Gran were battling their way in through the slushy water. The mourning dove from under the dome sat on Gran's arm. Mustard, too, came wading in, and Dr. Weedblossom in a muck-streaked coat of white.

"Gramp!" cried my sister as he swept her into his arms.

Dr. Weedblossom was skidding around the melting floor, studying the damage with interest. "Always thought houses shouldn't be made out of owlstone," he remarked.

"Hi, brother," I greeted Mustard, giving him our secret handshake. "Have any trouble getting the people out of the mine?"

"Naw. That Moonflower seed of your sister's worked like a charm. All we had to do was shine it like a flashlight, and it melted every owl we met. Just the way it melted the lock on our cell, and the bars. Boy, were those miners ever glad to be rescued! So was my dad."

"And so was I." Gramp beamed, putting one arm around me and one around Mustard.

The younger kid grinned. "Tim and Verity and Shelley and Lew did the risky part."

"But where's Fardels?" I wanted to know. "And what's happened to that Moonflower seed, by the way?"

"Fardels is rescuing the zoo animals. Raoul had 'em all slung back into the meat locker. As for that seed, just look—your grandmother is putting it to use!"

It was a joy to watch Gran, with the glowing seed in her fist, marching along the ballroom's walls, dissolving owls. She'd go up to a tall one, shine the seed in its face and cry, "Oh, go be a puddle, you corny thing, you!" The owl's head would nod and its whole body would slump, and it would flush down out of its uniform into a puddle.

Working her way down the line of owls, Gran arrived face to face with Mrs. Weedblossom. Gran stopped. She stared.

"Why, Ottoline!" she yelled.

"*Mother!*" Mrs. Weedblossom yelled back.

What went on? We gaped in amazement as the two women swooped into each other's arms. When Gran was able to talk again, she turned to Verity and me, her eyes wet with gladness, and she said, "Twins, don't you know who this it? It's your very own mother!"

I was so stunned I could have fallen through the floor. In fact, I almost did, because a great hole had opened up next to me. I gazed in wonder at Mrs. Weedblossom, who was doing the same to me. I'd always liked her a lot. But, so help me, this was too much to understand at the moment. I didn't know whether to laugh or cry.

As for Mustard, the kid was ogling me as if I

was something out of a flying saucer. "Timothy—
then you and I really *are* brothers?"

"We really are, I guess," I said dumbfoundedly.
Now I knew why, when Gran had first laid eyes
on Mustard, the younger kid had looked familiar
to her. He had mustard-colored hair and two-
colored eyes just like his mother. Just like *our*
mother, I mean.

NOTE BY VERITY: *In case you're wondering—years
ago when Timmy and I were babies, our father, Mr.
Tibb, had died. Then Mother had accidentally fallen
off the Cape May ferryboat and disappeared. But Gran
and Gramp hadn't ever given up hope of finding her.
They'd kept on looking. That was why Gramp had built
the catamaran. They had wanted to sail in the neighborhood of the ocean where Mother had last been seen.
Mother, of course, had fallen through a door at sea,
and she had been washed up in the Land of the Moonflower. There, she had soon met and married Dr. Weedblossom. So you see, Mustard was only our half-brother.
But he was as good as a whole one, any day.*

"For Pete's sake!" Lew Ladybug exploded, "save
the family reunion, will you? This whole joint is
falling down around our ears!"

"Let's blow, Ratty!" bellowed Raoul, grabbing
the fake baroness by the arm and splashing toward the door.

"Never mind them!" Dr. Weedblossom shouted.
"Outside, everyone! This house will collapse in a
minute and a half!"

But the Elders just milled in confusion. To add to the uproar, Fardels came busting in through a soggy wall, with the whole pack of romping, liberated animals at his heels. Ostriches, zebras and monkeys were slopping around in the slush, having a fine time, filling the room with bleating and honking and trumpeting.

But now the Grand Ballroom's floor was tilting down at a sharp angle. A river of slush was racing downhill toward the door. A few Elders struggled away in the door's direction, but waves crashed, knocking them off their feet. The floor was pitching like the deck of a boat getting ready to turn turtle. A wave slapped me across the shoulder and flicked off Lew. Now the detective was adrift on the surface of the water. Crooking a finger, I scooped him to safety and shook him off and set him back on my collar to dry.

But this was bad. I'd expected Lew to take command of us—to lead us out of the Hall. For the moment, the detective was too groggy. What to do? We were lost—unless somebody showed us the way.

Somebody?

Anybody. Even me!

Desperately, I shot a glance around the room. The only furniture that hadn't melted—it was wood and not owlstone—was the table a hundred feet long. Overturned, it lay on its back, legs up, floating like an island in the flood.

"THE TABLE!" I bawled. "Climb aboard the table, everybody!"

It took a lot of bawling to make myself heard. Dr. Weedblossom urged Mrs. Weedblossom—was she really my mother?—onto the table, and he sloshed through the hip-deep water and saw to Gran and Gramp. Mustard helped Verity. The two dozen Elders clambered aboard, and the brown bear rounded up the last of the struggling animals.

"We're leaving, Cressida!" I yelled to the water woman. "Can you flow along with us?"

"Right behind you, Timothy!" she chimed.

Then we took off. The ballroom floor propelled us. With a lurch, it pitched downward at a fierce slant, and the table started moving down a steep hill, like a loaded sled, bumping and jolting and gathering speed as it went. I was sitting up front like a captain, between the two front legs, but of course there was no way to steer. All I could do was shout, "Hang on, everybody!"— and hang on for dear life myself. At my back some of the Elders were screeching louder than the rhinos, cheetahs, and baboons.

As the table picked up momentum, carving a fast path through the water—which was bobbing with owl heads—cold slush sprayed past us left and right. Whooshing along like a comet, we shot out of the ballroom and down a corridor, making for the big front doors. They were bolted, but that didn't stop us. We shot right on through those two slabs of slush like a cannonball passing through a couple of bricks of butter.

Down over the front steps we sped. Cressida Pond flowed onward, by our side. Like a canoe shooting rapids, we went bounding along a dirt road that led down the mountainside. Rivers of melted owlstone thundered around us, helping to sweep our vessel on. We skimmed halfway down the mountain before the mud slowed us to a stop.

Fascinated, I gazed back up the mountainside. The stem of the Hall was twisted like a corkscrew. The roof drooped like a toadstool in the sun.

From under us, the ground gave a rumble. As if trying to shrug off something it could no longer stand, Moonflower Mountain was giving itself a final, heartfelt shake.

With a rubbery shudder, Owlstone Hall slithered clean off its foundations and went waddling out to the tip of the mountain's nose, dragging its ponderous factory. There, for a second, the huge house balanced, teetering back and forth. Then, like a ton of soft snow dropping off a rooftop in spring, it plunged on over the edge.

Silence.

Then a shivering BAA-AL-LL-LL-OOOO-MM-M-M!

I stared down into the valley. A mess of small

gray icebergs covered its floor. The giant toad-stool had burst to a thousand bits.

At the side of the road, a fragment of the owl-stone crown was melting. From the bottom of its puddle, something shone—one bright green cat's-eye jewel. All that remained of the Empire of Owlstonia. Somehow, even though I collect souvenirs, I didn't feel like stooping to pick it up.

20. *A Different Light*

Sprawled on my back in the warm grass, I watched the windmill moths paddling up and down the mountainside. Moonflower Mountain wasn't the only thing that had turned around. Just days ago, back in New Jersey, Verity and I had felt completely alone. But now we had family and friends galore.

Our picnic cloth had been spread on the shore of Cressida Pond. In her new home at the foot of the mountain, Cressida was once again so clear that you could see Finn and Fiona cruising around in her.

"No need," said my grandfather, thinking out loud, "no need to live under clouds or in shadow. Now, you young ones—all of us—can live by the sun and by the moon and by the Moonflower. By a light with a tinge of wonder to it. By a steady, clear, forgiving kind of light."

"Agamemnon," Gran said gently, reaching an arm around him, "sometimes I believe you love to hear yourself talk."

"Places, everyone!" cried Mother. "It's time for Fardels's cake!"

The birthday cake had wild honey frosting. On its top layer stood a miniature brown bear leading a column of animals. Last in line was a ribbon of green frosting. Boswell Boa Constrictor.

"That's the ss-ss-ss-spitting image of me," hissed the snake.

Verity's eyes were dancing behind the new glasses Dr. Weedblossom had made for her. "Listen up, will you? Shelley Snail has a fortune for Fardels!"

From the palm of my sister's hand came the poet and prophet's clear, small voice:

For. Fardels. Bear. And. All. Who. Hold. Him. Dear.
This. Day. Begins. One. Honey. Of. A. Year.

"Why," said my mother, "that includes everyone in the Land. And the animals. Fardels, you're doing a great job at the zoo. All the animals say they've never been so happy."

"They'd better say so, the bums," growled the bear, doffing a hat that said CHIEF KEEPER on it.

"And what about Lew?" my sister put in. "Isn't he doing a great job, too?"

Perched on a blade of grass, the Land of the Moonflower's Official Detective blushed redder under his spots. "Forget that stuff, angel," he rasped. "I do my job. Not that there's much crime around here these days."

It was true—the worst criminals had been banished. Raoul and Ratisha—somehow, I couldn't think of them by their real names—had been sent back to Earth to the Grimbles' parsnip farm. That had been the punishment the Elders had handed them. They had had to replace Verity and me at digging parsnips and licking labels and shipping the famous punch to its seventy thousand faithful sufferers. And I figured that Raoul and Ratisha and the Grimbles and Rouser ought to get along fine. Somehow, they all deserved each other.

Later that day, after the Elders had got together and elected Gramp one of them, he and I were collecting chestnuts on the mountainside. We stopped to look down over the trees, all golden and orange and red. High places still gave me a few cold shakes. But I was working on them.

All of a sudden a great rustling stole out of the air, and the sky glowed with a thousand wands of light. Gramp and I looked up to see the Moonflower unfolding its blossoms to the early-rising moon. It was as if a bunch of silver bonfires were burning on the mountainside. As if they'd been burning there since the opening day of time.

"Tell me something, Tim," said my grandfather. "You and Verity don't ever get homesick for Earth, do you?"

"No sir," I said truthfully. As far as I knew, we

hadn't even thought of that.

"Then you won't mind staying in this country"—he spoke his next word carefully—"*forever?*"

I picked up a chestnut and skimmed it down over the treetops and watched it disappear.

"I guess that will be long enough," I said.

About the Author

X. J. KENNEDY is the author of eight collections of poetry, three of them for children, including *One Winter Night in August* and *The Phantom Ice Cream Man. The Owlstone Crown* is his first novel. X. J. Kennedy and his wife, Dorothy, live with their five children in Bedford, Massachusetts, where they write textbooks and children's books together.